KAYLA O'BRIAN
AND THE RUNAWAY ORPHANS

Other Crossway Books by
Hilda Stahl

THE PRAIRIE FAMILY ADVENTURE SERIES

Sadie Rose and the Daring Escape
Sadie Rose and the Cottonwood Creek Orphan
Sadie Rose and the Outlaw Rustlers
Sadie Rose and the Double Secret
Sadie Rose and the Mad Fortune Hunters
Sadie Rose and the Phantom Warrior
Sadie Rose and the Champion Sharpshooter

THE SUPER J*A*M SERIES

The Great Adventures of Super J*A*M
The World's Greatest Hero

GROWING UP ADVENTURES

Sendi Lee Mason and the Milk Carton Kids
Sendi Lee Mason and the Stray Striped Cat
Sendi Lee Mason and the Big Mistake
Senid Lee Mason and the Great Crusade

KAYLA O'BRIAN ADVENTURES

Kayla O'Brian and the Dangerous Journey
Kayla O'Brian: Trouble at Bitter Creek Ranch
Kayla O'Brian and the Runaway Orphans

DAISY PUNKIN SERIES

Daisy Punkin
(more to follow)

A KAYLA O'BRIAN ADVENTURE

Kayla O'Brian
AND THE
RUNAWAY ORPHANS

Hilda Stahl

CROSSWAY BOOKS • WHEATON, ILLINOIS
A DIVISION OF GOOD NEWS PUBLISHERS

Kayla O'Brian and the Runaway Orphans.

Copyright © 1991 by Hilda Stahl.

Published by Crossway Books, a division of
Good News Publishers, Wheaton, Illinois 60187.

Series design: Ad Plus; Cover illustration: David Acquistapace

First printing, 1991

Printed in the United States of America

Library of Congress Cataloging-in-Publication Data
Stahl, Hilda
    Kayla O'Brian and the runaway orphans / Hilda Stahl
       p.   cm.— (Kayla O'Brian adventures)
    Summary: The Larsens have never celebrated Christmas on
their Nebraska mule farm; but this year, with the arrival of two
Christian orphans from the orphan train, seems meant to be
different.
    [1. Orphans—Fiction. 2. Frontier and pioneer life—Fiction.
3. West (U.S.)—Fiction. 4. Christian life—Fiction. 5.
Christmas—Fiction.] I. Title. II. Series: Stahl, Hilda. Kayla Obrian
adventures.
PZ7.S78244Kav 1991   [Fic]—dc20
11454
ISBN 0-89107-631-X

99		98		97		96		95		94		93		92		91
15	14	13	12	11	10	9	8	7	6	5	4	3	2	1

Dedicated
with love to
Donna Winters

Contents

Rachel's Announcement

Shivering with cold, Kayla O'Brian forked hay off the tall haystack at the side of the corral and pitched it over the fence for the mules. Suddenly a giant snowball splatted against the back of the ugly brown coat the Children's Aid Society had given her when she and her brother had first started west on the Orphan Train with orphans collected on the streets of New York City.

Kayla spun around just in time to see Timothy duck behind the granary with Brownie at his side. "'Tis a fight you want, Timothy O'Brian?" Kayla laughed, and her blue eyes twinkled. The early-morning sky was gray, and a December chill hung in the air. "Come out and fight like a man, Timothy O'Brian!" she called as she scooped up a handful of snow and packed it into a ball.

"I'll get him for you!" called Jane Larsen with a giggle as she ran from the big barn. She was tall for eleven years . . . and lean. She wore cowboy boots, a gray heavy winter coat with a black woolen scarf around her neck, and a drooping cowboy hat on her head. She scooped up snow and ran to the far side of the granary. "I'll get you, Timothy!"

"I'm that ready to take on all of you!" shouted Timothy, pressing against the side of the granary, his cheeks red and his blue eyes flashing with excitement. Brownie looked up at him and whined and waved his bushy light-brown tail.

Jane squealed as Timothy pitched a snowball at her. Kayla laughed. It was good to see Jane laughing and playing. When Kayla and Timothy had first come off the Orphan Train to live with the Larsens, the entire family had been unsmiling and sad. Rachel and Abel Larsen said many times that Kayla and Timothy had brought happiness into their lives. Because Abel was laid up from being kicked by a mule, Rachel had gone to meet the Orphan Train. She'd chosen them even though Abel had sent her after a tall, strapping boy. Timothy was thirteen and was impatiently waiting for his growth spurt. Even eleven-year-old Jane was taller than Timothy.

Just then, with a shy smile Greene Larsen stepped up to Kayla. He was fifteen and already as big as a man. "I'll protect you, Kayla." He flung a snowball at the granary, and it spattered against the gray wood.

Kayla smiled impishly at Greene, then reached up and pushed a handful of snow into the back of his heavy coat collar, just below the broad brim of his hat.

Greene turned and looked at her in great surprise, but then his face softened, and love shone from his dark eyes.

Kayla's pulse leaped. She wondered what it would feel like for him to kiss her. Someday she knew he would, but she wasn't ready yet. She smiled at him. He reached for her, but ducked, scooped up a snowball, and ran away with it.

Suddenly a snowball splatted against her back. She glanced back just as Greene threw another snowball that hit her chest and sprayed into her flushed face. She laughed and threw her snowball at Greene, but he ducked, and the snowball flew into the corral with the mules. "I'll get you next time, Greene Larsen!" she shouted. Her voice rang across the vast snow-covered Nebraska prairie.

Just then six-year-old Ula shouted out the door of the house, "Breakfast is on! Come and get it!"

"Race you!" shouted Timothy. Kayla spun around, skidded on packed snow, and fell flat. Before she could jump up Greene lifted her and brushed her off.

"Are you hurt?" he asked in great concern, his dark eyes clouded with emotion.

"Not a bit! 'Twould take more than a fall in soft snow to hurt the likes of me." Kayla pulled off her scarf and flipped her mass of long black hair back. "Race you, Greene!"

He laughed, a sound that pleased her. It still didn't come easy for him, nor did talking, but he was getting better at both.

She leaped forward, careful this time of her footing. Together they ran past the shed and the toilet to the long wrap-around front porch on the two-story white frame house. Kayla caught the door before it closed after Jane and Timothy and stepped directly into the large kitchen. The heat smote her, and she peeled off her coat and hung it on a peg near the door. Snow scattered across the wooden floor from her boots. She smiled at the others already sitting at the oblong table. Abel Larsen sat at the head of the table and Rachel at the foot. Five-year-old Scott sat to Rachel's left. Ula stood at the kitchen range and stuck a chunk of wood in it. Smells of pancakes, eggs, coffee, and hot syrup made Kayla's stomach cramp with hunger.

"I'm hungry enough to eat a . . . a mule," said Timothy with a laugh as he sat down. He and Kayla had thought they were going to live on a ranch with horses, but instead, much to his dismay, they learned the Larsens raised mules. Timothy knew horses, but not mules. He was still trying to tolerate the mules.

Kayla sat between Timothy and Ula and across from Greene, Jane, and Scott. She quickly folded her hands in her lap and bowed her head while Abel said the blessing over the food and the family. None of the family had prayed before Kayla and Timothy came to live with them. Kayla was thankful they'd all accepted Jesus as Savior and were learning to be like Him.

"I want a sled for Christmas," said Scott as he waited for the plate of eggs to reach him.

Rachel frowned as she forked pancakes onto her plate. She was tall and slim with a long, thin, plain face. Her dark blonde hair was pulled back into a bun at the nape of her long neck. "What makes you think you'll get anything for Christmas?" asked Rachel sharply.

"Kayla said so," said Scott, his round face red.

"Christmas is just another day. We don't celebrate Christmas like other folks, and we never will," said Rachel in a dead voice.

Kayla almost choked on the pancake in her mouth. Had she heard Rachel right? Kayla glanced at Timothy and saw he was as shocked as she was, but Greene and Jane weren't at all surprised. Scott and Ula looked ready to burst into tears. Abel lifted a brow and studied Rachel without speaking.

"Ma!" cried Scott. "Kayla said we'd get presents and decorate a tree and everything!"

"She said Santa Claus would come to our house," whispered Ula.

"I didn't say there was a Santa Claus," said Kayla. "I only told you the stories I heard."

Rachel Larsen turned steel-blue eyes on Kayla. "Since when are you the boss on this ranch, Kayla O'Brian?"

Kayla swallowed hard, then lifted her chin. "'Tis not the boss I am, Rachel. 'Tis a member of the family I am, but with a different last name."

"Christmas is a time to celebrate," said Timothy, determined to stick up for his sister just as she always did for him. He was thirteen and Kayla fourteen. "We always celebrate Christmas."

"*We* don't," snapped Rachel. "What is there to celebrate?"

"I thought you'd want to," said Kayla. "'Tis only right to celebrate the birth of Jesus."

"We never gave gifts before, and we won't start now!" Rachel picked up her cup of coffee as if to say the conversation was over.

Abel Larsen cleared his throat as he looked down the cluttered table at his wife. "Rachel, it's not for you to decide if we have gifts or don't have gifts."

Rachel stiffened. "I never heard you say a word about Christmas all these years."

"More's the pity," said Abel. "But I'm saying it now. We need to put aside a day to celebrate Jesus and to show we care for each other."

"That we do," said Kayla.

"I won't agree to hard-earned money used for frivolous

gifts!" said Rachel coldly. "If you plan to have this celebration, you'll do it without me."

Kayla gasped, but Rachel went back to eating as if she hadn't shattered everyone's happy plans.

Abel leaned forward. "Rachel, we'll talk about this later."

"Talk all you want, but I won't change my mind." Rachel poured more syrup on her pancakes, poked the egg yoke to make it run over the syrup, then cut a bite of pancake and egg.

Kayla's heart sank, but then she remembered that God was with her in every situation. With a confident smile Kayla looked at Rachel. God was a God of miracles. He'd already worked one miracle in Rachel, and He could surely work another one. "'Tis not going to take much money, Rachel. You'll see."

"Finish your breakfast. You and Timothy are taking Ma to town later."

Kayla's eyes lit up, and she shot a look at Timothy. He was just as excited.

Abel frowned. "When did this come about?"

"I talked to Ma about it last night while I helped her with her chores," said Rachel. "She needs a few supplies, and I told her I'd send Kayla and Timothy over."

Abel shrugged. "You two take the wagon. Be careful and watch the weather. If it starts snowing you hightail it for home."

"We will," said Timothy.

"They'll be safe with Ma," said Rachel stiffly.

Kayla nodded. She'd been afraid of Pansy Butler and her collie Czar when she'd first met them, but now they were friends. It felt good to have a grandma again. Pansy was hungry for someone to read to her and talk to her. She told Kayla all she knew about Russia, and Kayla told her all she knew about Ireland and New York City.

Timothy finished his last bite of pancake, drained his glass of milk, then excused himself. "I'll hitch up the wagon, Kayla. Come out when you've finished eating." He wanted to get out before Abel decided Greene should go instead.

"I'll change my clothes and be right out," said Kayla.

"No need to do that," said Rachel sharply. "You're going to get supplies for Ma, not to impress someone. Go as you are."

Flushing, Kayla reluctantly nodded, then finished eating. She wondered, was Boon Russell still in Spade? She'd hate for him to see her looking ragged and ugly. She frowned. She'd just plain hate to see him.

A Trip to Town

Just as Kayla reached the wagon, Abel called to her. Surprised, she turned to see him walking toward her, leaning heavily on his cane. It was still very hard for him to get around in the snow. He looked ready to burst with excitement. His wide-brimmed hat sat on the back of his head, showing blond hair at his forehead. His dark blue coat hung over his lean frame, down almost to his worn cowboy boots. He hadn't bothered to slip on his gloves.

"What does he want?" muttered Timothy with a scowl as he gripped the reins tightly. His breath hung in the air.

Kayla ran back to Abel, her dark brow raised questioningly. As he caught Kayla's hand in his, Abel whispered, "Take this money and buy a brooch for Rachel."

Kayla darted a look toward the house. "She'll get mad."

"I know, but I'm getting it anyway. Don't even let Timothy know. I don't want the secret out until Christmas." Abel pushed the folded bills down into Kayla's glove. It bit into her palm.

"What brooch?" Kayla whispered, shivering with

excitement. She knew it was hard for Abel to stand up to Rachel since he'd let her be the boss of the ranch and of him until just lately. "What does it look like?"

"There's one in the general store. I saw her looking at it when she didn't know I saw." Abel grinned. "She puts on a hard act at times, but underneath she's a soft woman."

"I know." Kayla had learned that very thing, and it had surprised her. "Tell me what the brooch looks like."

"It's silver, carved all fancy to look like a doily. And it has a big amethyst set in it. It's about as big as a silver dollar." Abel suddenly looked nervous. "But if that one's gone, get another one. I know you can choose one Rachel would like."

Kayla nodded and whispered, "I'll do it."

Abel bent his head down close to Kayla, and she smelled his coffee breath. "Don't let anyone know or anyone see it but me."

Kayla lifted her chin high. "I give my word as an O'Brian."

"We've heard that a lot since you and Timothy came," said Abel with a chuckle. "And we all know O'Brians keep their word."

"That we do!" said Kayla, her cheeks pink.

Abel laughed and patted Kayla's shoulder, then sobered. "Be careful in town. There's always drifters going through this time of year lookin' for work. If they know you have that much money on you, they'd want it and would take it however they could."

"Nobody will get this money from me! I'll buy the brooch and bring it back safe and sound."

"Thanks, Kayla." Abel hugged her, then let her go. "See you before dark."

Kayla smiled at him as she remembered how she'd thought he was mean when first she'd met him, but now she knew he was kind and thoughtful. He wanted to turn the ranch into a horse ranch as well as a mule ranch. Kayla and Timothy were thankful for that.

"If you see anything that looks like a Christmas tree, cut it down and bring it home," said Abel. "There's a small saw in the toolbox in the wagon."

"We'll do what we can." With an excited laugh Kayla ran to the wagon and climbed up on the high seat beside Timothy. She huddled into her ugly brown coat and tightened the woolen scarf around her head and neck. The mules were patiently waiting, but Kayla could tell by Timothy's face that he was far from patient.

"What's wrong, Timothy?" she asked as he slapped the reins and clucked to the mules.

Timothy kept his eyes straight ahead. "Did he want Greene to come instead of me?"

"He never said a word about that!"

Timothy was quiet until they drove around the first low hill away from Bitter Creek Ranch. He felt the question burning inside him, and finally he blurted out, "He doesn't think I'm going to grow, does he?"

Kayla frowned as she braced her feet on the wagon bed. "Timothy O'Brian, what is it you're thinking?"

A muscle jumped in Timothy's cheek. "He wants to send me back to the Orphan Train."

"That he does not!"

"Then what was it he was saying to you?"

Kayla started to tell Timothy, then shook her head. "That I can't be telling. 'Tis a secret."

A dark cloud settled over Timothy's face, and he

slapped the reins harder on the mules. He was sure Abel liked Greene better than him. Sometimes he wondered if Kayla did too. She was starting to act funny around Greene. A hard knot tightened in Timothy's stomach. He wanted to talk to Kayla about it, but he was afraid he might start bawling. A boy of thirteen was too old for that. "You used to tell me everything."

Kayla frowned at him. "What's gotten into you, Timothy O'Brian? You can't be wanting me to tell a secret! An O'Brian would never tell a secret!"

"Sometimes 'tis hard to be an O'Brian, Kayla!" snapped Timothy. "I wish Mama and Papa were alive and we were all living together on Briarwood Farms in Maryland! We'd be training horses with Papa."

Tears sprang to Kayla's eyes, but she quickly blinked them away. "That I wish too, Timothy, but we live on a mule ranch instead." She managed a bright smile. "But thanks to you we have three good horses now and are training them."

Timothy sighed heavily. The rattle of the harness and the crunch of the snow under the wheels were the only sounds in the vast prairie. The gray sky stretched on and on and was lost as it blended with the snowy hills.

Kayla laid her hand on Timothy's as she looked at him. His raven-black hair hung too long below the wide brim of his new hat. She should've cut his hair two days ago when she'd cut Greene's, but when she'd called him, he'd not answered, and then she'd forgotten. "Our lives aren't what we wanted, Timothy, but we're where we are, and God is with us." She grinned. "Even on a mule ranch."

"I know," said Timothy stiffly. "But I can't help wishing things were different. I wish I was as tall and strong as Papa right now! I'm tired of waiting!"

"I know. I know. But you'll grow, Timothy . . . Just as I did on the trip from Ireland." Kayla swallowed hard to ease the lump in her throat. She'd left County Offaly a girl, but on the trip she'd grown into a woman.

Kayla glanced off across the snow-covered rolling hills. The folded money poked into her palm, and she wanted to lift her skirt and slip it into the hidden pocket of her petticoat. She peeked through her long dark lashes at Timothy. He was staring straight ahead, his face set. Maybe she should tell him about the brooch Abel wanted her to buy for Rachel. Kayla shook her head. She couldn't tell. She'd promised not to. Nothing could drag it out of her, not even Timothy.

Finally Timothy stopped the mules near the porch at Pansy Butler's house. Czar barked inside the house. Timothy glanced toward the small sod chicken house, the large wooden barn, and the other outbuildings. He looked past the toilet to the fenced-in cemetery plot where Pansy's seven babies were buried. Only Rachel had lived. Pansy's husband had died a few years ago, and he was buried there too, his marker taller than the others.

Timothy glanced toward the house. He knew Rachel would be over later to do the chores since Pansy Butler was not strong enough to do them herself.

Suddenly the door opened, and Pansy stepped out onto the porch. She hoisted the gunbelt onto her round hips and told Czar to stop barking. The big gold and white collie sank to the porch with his head on his paws, his eyes on Pansy. One command from her and Czar would rip an intruder to bits.

Pansy smiled, and her eyes were almost lost in the deep wrinkles on her face. She hugged her shawl closer around her thick shoulders. "I can't go with you kids today," she said in her raspy voice.

"Are you sick?" asked Kayla, jumping down to the snowy ground. She ran up on the porch and peered down at Pansy. Kayla felt like a tall thin giant next to the short, round woman. "What can I do for you?"

"Take my list and money and get my supplies for me," said Pansy.

"We've never gone to Spade alone," said Timothy. Why hadn't he kept his mouth shut! Now maybe she'd send them back to Bitter Creek Ranch and have Greene go in his place.

"You know the way, don't you?" snapped Pansy in her sharp manner.

Timothy nodded.

"Then you won't get lost."

Timothy grinned and suddenly felt better.

Pansy turned back to Kayla. "You can get my things and come back home. It's as easy as that."

"We'll do it," said Kayla. Pansy gave Kayla the list and some money in a crumpled envelope. "You pin that in your petticoat pocket right now!"

Kayla turned her back to Timothy, lifted her skirt, and tucked the envelope in her pocket. Cold wind blew against her legs, chilling her even through the long underwear Rachel had given her to wear. She quickly slipped the money from Abel inside her pocket too, pinned the pocket shut, and dropped her skirt back in place.

Pansy jabbed Kayla's arm. "You bring back the change. Don't spend even a penny of it or I'll know."

Kayla stood to her fullest height, and sparks flew from her blue eyes. Her long, flowing jet-black hair seemed to crackle with indignation. "O'Brians don't steal! Not even a penny!"

Czar lifted his head and whined. Pansy chuckled and slapped Kayla's back. "Didn't mean to hurt your feelings, girl! It's downright hard for me to remember you never do anything wrong. It's beyond me."

"I never said we were perfect," said Kayla in a small voice.

"You just never do anything wrong," said Pansy.

Kayla pressed her lips tightly together. She didn't want to talk about her faults and give Satan credit. The day she'd accepted Jesus as her Savior, she'd become a new creature in Christ. With God's help she was learning to be like Jesus. She would not talk about her long lists of faults, even when she was goaded and teased about being perfect.

"We'd better get going," said Timothy as he looked at the overcast sky. "We don't want to get caught in a blizzard."

Kayla bent down and hugged Pansy, patted Czar's great head, then ran back to the wagon. She climbed up beside Timothy and said breathlessly, "I'm ready."

Lifting his cowboy hat, Timothy smiled at Pansy. "We'll be back before dark, Pansy." She'd asked them to call her that until she could get used to them calling her Grandma the way her real grandchildren did.

Timothy called to the two brown mules. They stepped forward carefully, and the wagon rolled out into the prairie away from Pansy's ranch. It was a couple of miles to Spade. There wasn't a road across Pansy's pasture, but Timothy knew by the shape of the hills which way to go. Finally they reached the narrow dirt trail that was the road.

As they drew closer to Spade, Kayla's stomach fluttered with butterflies. Would Boon Russell still be in town, or had he gone back to Vermont where he lived? He'd been trying to earn enough money to go home to his mother and father. Kayla bit her bottom lip. If Boon was in town, would he even look at her, or was he still infatuated with redheaded Clare from the Orphan Train?

Shopping

Kayla shivered as Timothy drew closer to Spade. Dare she look toward the Petres' place to see if she could see Clare? Kayla heard the squawk of the windmill and the bawling of cattle over the soft hoofbeats of the mules, the rattle of the wagon, and the wild beat of her heart.

A cowboy rode past on a big sorrel that Kayla knew Timothy admired. Papa had taught her and Timothy how to judge good horseflesh and how to train horses. Timothy would know right off that the cowboy's sorrel was special.

"I'd like to be as big as that cowboy," said Timothy gruffly.

Kayla shook her head in surprise. She'd expected him to comment on the sorrel. "Timothy, get your mind off your size. You're a fine lad. Be thinking on that!"

Timothy scowled harder. He was tired of thinking on that. He was going to be fourteen May 1st. If he was still a short, skinny boy then, he didn't know what he'd do.

Kayla finally found the courage to glance toward the Petre place. The wide front yard was full of snow. A tall snowman wearing a cowboy hat stood beside a giant cotton-wood tree. The pasture beside the barn seemed full of cows. Kayla knew the people from town kept their milk cows there. Twice a day someone from each family would come milk his cow. They paid the Petres for feeding, watering, and caring for the cows. Kayla turned to look at the big white house. She couldn't see anyone, not even a movement behind the curtains in the windows. Trembling, she looked ahead. At the sight of the livery her stomach cramped. Boon had worked there the last time they were in town.

Moving with the sway of the wagon, Kayla locked her hands in her lap as she watched the wide doorway of the livery. No one was in sight. She looked at the corral, but saw only horses and no men. Maybe Boon had gone back to Vermont.

Across the frozen dirt-packed street she saw the black-smith shop with horses in a corral in back. The smell of wood smoke filled the air. The ring of hammer on anvil was louder than the creak of the wagon.

Kayla glanced at the harness and saddle shop, but no one was in sight there either. Inside the wide window of the feed and grain she caught a glimpse of several men standing with the proprietor. Three saddled horses stood tied to the wooden hitchrail.

"There aren't many folks in town today," said Timothy.

"The kids are probably in school," said Kayla, looking longingly at the schoolhouse at the end of the street, across from the small white church. She missed going to school almost as much as she missed going to church. Rachel said it was too far to go to either, especially in the winter.

Timothy stopped in front of the general store just as a wagon pulled by a team of brown workhorses drove toward them. The clop of the hooves and the rattle of the wagon sounded loud on the quiet street. Timothy jumped down and tied the mules to the hitchrail. He frowned at the mules. Would he ever be able to drive a team of mules without being embarrassed?

Kayla climbed carefully to the ground. She wanted to jump down the way she usually did, but she didn't want anyone, especially Boon, to see her acting unladylike. She walked into the general store, and the bell over the door tinkled. Heat from the potbelly stove struck her, and the smells made her wrinkle her nose. Quickly she pulled off her scarf and gloves.

"Howdy," said the owner, Ivan Polaski, from behind the counter. He was of medium build, with brown hair and eyes and the biggest nose Kayla had ever seen.

"Hello," said Kayla.

"It's mighty cold out. Cold enough to freeze your words in midair."

"That it is!" answered Kayla with a laugh.

Polaski's face lit up. "I know you! I couldn't place you at first, but when you talked I knew. You're the Irish orphan the Larsens took in."

Kayla flushed. How she hated to be called an orphan!

Just then Timothy walked in, his cheeks and nose red from the cold.

"Howdy, young fella," said Polaski with a wide smile. "You're the other Irish orphan, aren't you?"

Timothy managed not to snap out in anger as he nodded. "We came to buy supplies for Pansy Butler."

"You let me know what I can do to help," said Polaski just as the door opened and a man walked in with a big boxer dog beside him.

"Can't have dogs in here, Deems," said Polaski as he hurried around the counter, frowning at the big brown and black dog.

"Box goes where I go," snapped the man, pulling off his wide-brimmed hat to scratch his shaggy dark hair.

Kayla ducked around a counter of folded shirts and pants and walked to the counter where she saw the jewelry. As the men argued about the dog and Timothy looked at rifles, Kayla looked at the brooches. She found the silver one with the amethyst. It was a real beauty, all right. She darted a look around to make sure no one saw her, then carefully lifted her skirt and unpinned her pocket to get Pansy's envelope and Abel's money.

Swearing angrily, the man finally put his dog outdoors, then walked to the shelves of canned goods.

Polaski walked back behind the counter, his face flushed and his eyes flashing with anger.

Kayla motioned for him to help her.

"Did you find something you want?" he asked, trying to sound cheerful again.

"That brooch," she said, pointing to the silver and amethyst jewelry.

"Fine choice," Polaski said as he lifted it out of the display case. He named the price, and Kayla paid him. She handed him Pansy's list, and he walked away to fill it while Kayla quickly pinned the brooch into her hidden pocket.

"What're you doing, Kayla?" asked Timothy.

She turned with a flush. "I didn't see you."

He looked at her with a frown, then whispered, "That man has a load of kids in the back of his wagon. Come look."

Kayla followed Timothy to the front window and

looked out. The kids in the wagon looked cold and frightened. "I wonder who they are," she whispered.

"I don't know," whispered Timothy. "I'll talk to them when we go out."

Just then Polaski called, "Your order's ready, kids."

Timothy picked up the box while Kayla paid. She wanted to pin the money in her pocket in privacy, so she said, "I'll meet you in the wagon, Timothy. I want to go out back first."

With the few coins in her hand, Kayla turned and bumped into the man who had the dog.

"Watch where you're walkin'," he snapped.

"I'm that sorry," she said.

The man scowled at her. "You Irish should've stayed in Ireland where you belong! Your kind is givin' America a bad name."

Bright flags of red flew in her cheeks, and fire shot from her blue eyes. "Sir, not one word will you speak against Ireland or against me!"

The man brushed her aside as if she were a flea on his dog.

Kayla choked back her angry words as she walked out the back door. Just then she caught a movement at the toilet, then a flash of flapping skirts as a girl ran from the corner of the toilet to hide behind a big cottonwood tree. Kayla frowned. Was the girl playing hide and seek?

Kayla heard a sound nearby, and she glanced toward the rain barrel. A small black boy was crouched down between the rain barrel and the store. His eyes were wide with fright. Kayla started to speak, but he looked so frightened that she didn't. Thoughtfully she walked to the toilet. The door was locked from the outside, so she knew it was unoccupied. She started to turn the wooden latch, but stopped when she heard a strange noise inside. Her stomach tightened.

"Is someone locked in?" she asked. There was no answer, so cautiously she turned the latch and opened the door. The big boxer dog lay on his side, his mouth tied shut with a scarf and a small rope looped around his feet. She gasped. The boxer growled low in his throat. Kayla swallowed hard.

Quickly she looked around, but no one was in sight. She lifted the dog out of the toilet. "Who did this to you?" she asked softly as she worked on the rope. She untied his feet, then pulled off the scarf. He hesitated, and she stood very still. Would he bite her?

The dog whined and licked her hand. "I hope you didn't get hurt," she said softly as she patted the dog's head.

With a low bark the dog ran around the store, then barked louder.

Kayla stepped back inside the toilet and quickly pinned Pansy's money in place.

A few minutes later Kayla walked around the store. The boxer was barking, and the man who owned him was yelling at the top of his lungs. Suddenly frightened, Kayla stopped at the corner of the store. Frantically she looked for Timothy, but he wasn't on their wagon or standing beside it. Where was he?

Polaski shook the man's arm. "Calm down, mister! What're you carryin' on about?"

"All them kids are gone!" The man jerked away from Polaski. "I don't have all day to hunt down them kids. I got to be in North Platte before dark."

Her heart racing, Kayla backed out of sight. She could

feel in her bones that something dreadful was wrong. She thought of the boxer bound in the toilet, the girl ducking behind the cottonwood, and the boy hiding behind the rain barrel. Maybe the boy could answer her questions.

Kayla ran around the store and stopped at the rain barrel. The boy was gone. She frowned as she looked all around. She saw the backs of the stores and the outbuildings. Further away were the homes of the shopkeepers.

Her heart in her mouth, Kayla walked slowly around the store. Where was Timothy?

The Search

Her spine tingling, Kayla ran around the store and stopped beside her wagon. An icy gust of wind send shivers over her, and she hugged her coat to her. Where was Timothy? She saw the box of supplies for Pansy in the back of the wagon, but Timothy still wasn't in sight. The man, his dog, and Polaski weren't in sight either. The town looked even more deserted than it had earlier. She heard the restless movements of the mules and the ring of a hammer on an anvil at the blacksmith's. "Where are you, Timothy?" she whispered.

Kayla's mouth turned bone-dry. Her breath hung in the cold air. She ran to the general store and pushed the door open. The smell of wood smoke and hot air rushed out. Polaski looked up from reading a newspaper behind the counter. "Have you seen my brother?" Kayla asked in a tight voice.

"Not since he left," said Polaski. "Deems thinks he might've helped the load of orphans get away."

Kayla gasped. "What orphans?"

"From the wagon." Wrinkling his huge nose, Polaski

jabbed his thumb in the direction of the street. "Deems gets orphans where he can and takes them around to places far away from the railroad and finds homes for them orphans. He's not always kind to 'em, but he does get them homes, or he takes them to the workhouse down in Kansas."

Kayla trembled. Workhouse! She'd heard of the long, terrible hours kids had to work there. If they didn't obey, they were whipped and at times starved. She could understand why Timothy would help the orphans escape. "If my brother comes in, please be good enough to tell him I'm looking for him."

"Sure will," said Polaski, bending over his newspaper again.

The brooch bumping against her leg, Kayla walked toward the church and school, but she couldn't spot anyone. She heard singing from the school and yearned to walk inside and join in. Reluctantly she turned back and looked down the narrow dirt street toward the livery. She trembled. Could she walk to the livery to ask about Timothy? Her pulse pounded in her ears. What would she say to Boon if she saw him?

Kayla lifted her chin and squared her shoulders. An O'Brian was not a coward! With a firm stride Kayla walked to the livery stable. Just as she began to step inside, Deems and his boxer stepped out. His blue eyes flashing fire, Deems looked ready to burst with rage. He badly needed a bath, a shave, and a change of clothes. The dog licked Kayla's hand, and she patted his head.

"How are you, fella?" said Kayla softly, her hand on the dog's head.

"Box!" snarled Deems. "Get away from her!" He glared at Kayla. "Irish, see any kids around here?"

Kayla shook her head. She hadn't seen anyone around the livery, so she wasn't telling a lie. She heard a horse snort from inside the livery.

With a menacing step Deems stepped closer to Kayla. "You better not be helpin' them orphans run away from me or you'll end up in the workhouse yourself!"

Kayla squared her shoulders and looked Deems right in the eye. "Don't be threatenin' me, sir!"

"You're too sassy for your own good, Irish!" Deems looked around, then grinned wickedly. "We're all alone. No one would come to your rescue if I decided to take some of that sass out of you."

Kayla knotted her fists at her sides. She was trembling on the inside, but she wouldn't let it show. "Don't lay one hand on me, sir, or you'll be a sorry man!"

Just then Boon Russell stepped around the corner of the livery. Kayla's legs almost gave way. Boon's bright red hair looked even brighter against the drab winter colors around him. He looked from Deems to Kayla. "Need help, Kayla?"

"Not a bit!" she said, forcing her heart to stop racing like a runaway horse.

Swearing under his breath, Deems stalked down the street, Box at his heels.

"What'd he want?" asked Boon as he pushed his wide-brimmed hat to the back of his head. He looked much different dressed in work pants and a heavy coat lined with sheepskin than when she'd first found him hurt on the prairie dressed in his city clothes.

"He was looking for some runaway orphans," said Kayla. Could he hear the wild beat of her heart? She had once seen him kissing Clare, and he'd hurt her terribly. Why should she find it hard to breathe with him standing so near? She managed to keep her voice level. "And I'm lookin' for Timothy. Have you seen him about?"

Boon glanced toward Deems as he strode toward the general store, then back at Kayla. "He's hiding with some of the kids."

Kayla fell back a step, her hand at the knot of her scarf on her throat. "What?"

"See for yourself." Boon led the way, and Kayla followed him through the livery past several stalls to the back door of the tack room. She ignored the smell of manure and the mouse she saw race to a hiding place behind a pile of hay.

"Are you helping the orphans?" Kayla asked in surprise as they walked. She had learned what a selfish nature Boon had.

Boon nodded grimly. "I've seen Deems come through town before with a load of kids. He's mean to them." Boon lowered his voice. "Sometimes he kidnaps kids right from their homes so he can sell them somewhere else."

"Sell them?" asked Kayla, her hand at her throat again, her blue eyes wide.

Boon nodded again. "There are folks who'd pay to have free help."

"Why doesn't anyone stop Deems?"

"Nobody listens to the kids. They figure they're lying."

Kayla looked closely at Boon. She saw a look of concern on his face that surprised but pleased her. "But you do believe them."

"I can usually tell when someone is lying." He flushed and ducked his head.

A muscle jumped in Kayla's jaw. "'Twas you who lied about coming to see me after you left."

Boon reluctantly nodded.

"But why?" cried Kayla, her cheeks flushed as bright as Boon's hair.

"You wanted me to say yes so much that I couldn't break your heart."

With a low moan Kayla turned her back to Boon. How she wanted to run from him to hide her shame!

"I didn't mean to embarrass you, Kayla."

"Please don't speak of it further," she said just above a whisper. "That I could not bear."

Boon sighed heavily. "I'll take you to Timothy and the others."

How she wanted to run from him, but she followed him to a haystack outside the corral.

"Timothy," said Boon softly. "It's Boon. I have your sister with me."

"Kayla," said Timothy, his voice muffled. Boon pulled away a pile of hay to reveal a large hollowed-out place in the haystack. Timothy was crouched inside with three others—two girls and a boy. They looked cold and frightened.

"Deems has come and gone, but he might be back," said Boon.

"Timothy," said Kayla, suddenly at a loss for words. He stepped out, his eyes twinkling and a saucy grin on his face. He looked like he did when he'd survived the streets of New York City by his wits.

"Kayla, I want you to meet the Duval girls—Marigold and Beryl—and Abbott Belmont."

Kayla stared at the two girls and the boy. They seemed about her age. Marigold had long, light-red hair, and she glared at Kayla with wide blue eyes as she huddled next to the others. Beryl looked ready to cry as she stared at Kayla.

The girl nervously pushed back her tangled brown hair and blinked her brown eyes. The boy was much bigger than Timothy and badly needed a haircut. His face was dirty. He winked at Kayla, and she bit back a gasp of surprise.

"What will they do now?" asked Kayla, stepping closer to Timothy.

"They don't know," said Timothy. "Abb here was running away from the folks he lived with because they beat and starved him. Deems found him, and Abb thought it would be good to go with him, but then he found out the kind of man Deems is."

"I tried to get away," said Abb with a nod.

"Marigold and Beryl were taken from the Orphan Train over a month ago by a man who said he had a wife and kids, but was really a bachelor. The girls ran away, and Deems found them and promised to get them to a good home. They heard he was taking them to work in a saloon in Ogallala, so they ran, but he caught them," said Boon.

"He won't catch us again," said Marigold grimly. She glared at Kayla. "Don't you tell him or you'll be very sorry!"

Kayla opened her mouth to speak, but Timothy said, "You can trust Kayla."

"I hope so," said Marigold, still looking very suspicious. Kayla touched Timothy's arm. "'Tis late, Timothy. We must be getting home."

"I told the girls and Abb we'd take them with us," said Timothy.

Kayla gasped. "'Tis a foolish act, Timothy O'Brian!"

Timothy stared at Kayla in surprise. He'd never expected to hear her say that. "I thought you'd want to help them."

"I will help them all I can, Timothy, but what of Rachel and Abel? They won't let them stay at the ranch."

"Pansy might let them stay with her."

Kayla shook her head. "That she won't! She likes her life with only Czar to be looking out for."

"We must do something for them," said Timothy firmly.

"Don't bother with us," said Marigold sharply while Beryl whimpered into her hands. "We'll take care of ourselves."

"Just cover us back up until after dark," said Abb with a scowl.

Boon started putting the hay back in place, but Timothy caught his arm.

"They're going with us," said Timothy. "I'll bring the wagon."

Kayla gasped and stared at Timothy in surprise. What was wrong with him? He'd always obeyed her. "Timothy O'Brian, you cannot take them to the ranch!"

Timothy lifted his chin and looked very determined. "Kayla, I will take them with us. I gave my word."

"You'll have to break it," snapped Kayla, suddenly angry at Timothy. Why was he being so obnoxious, and especially in front of Boon?

Timothy shook his head. "An O'Brian does not break his word!"

"An O'Brian does not disobey!"

"You're not my mother, Kayla O'Brian, so stop acting like you are." Timothy turned his back to Kayla and said, "I'll be right back with the wagon."

Kayla clenched her fists at her sides as anger burned inside her.

Caught

Kayla grabbed Timothy's arm, but he shook off her hand and ran around the livery to get the wagon. Kayla whirled on Boon and shook her finger at him. "You did this to him! Him always so obedient and respectful."

Boon frowned as he took a step toward Kayla. His breath hung between them in the cold air. "I didn't talk Tim into anything."

"Tim! His name is Timothy, and don't be calling him Tim!" Kayla's legs trembled as she glared at Boon Russell. She felt as if she were standing off to the side watching this strange person who looked just like she did, but didn't act like she did at all.

Boon turned away from Kayla and reached down to help the girls out of the haystack. "Hide inside the tack room until Timothy gets here," Boon said. "And don't make any noise. I'll let you know when to come out."

Suddenly Kayla thought about the minister of the church. She'd never met him, but she was sure he'd help if he knew the situation. She strode purposefully through the livery. Yes, she'd get the minister to help, and then she and Timothy would be free to go home.

"Where do you think you're going, Kayla?" asked Boon sharply, his brown eyes narrowed into mere slits.

Kayla brushed back her scarf. "To tell the minister what's happening! He'll take care of the orphans."

Boon leaped forward and gripped Kayla's arm. "He won't help! We already tried. He believes Deems."

Kayla looked down at Boon's once white, well-manicured hand that was now as work-roughened as hers. His nails were cracked and dirty. She pried at his fingers, but he wouldn't release her. "Let me go!" she cried.

"Stop acting this way! It's not like you at all!"

She knew that, but she couldn't help herself.

"You're still angry because I led you on," said Boon in a low, tight voice. "I made you think we were falling in love with each other, but we weren't. You're a beautiful woman and you have a lot of spunk, but I'm not ready to settle with just one woman."

Kayla's face burned. Could the others hear Boon? It would be too humiliating if they did! "Let me go," Kayla whispered hoarsely. "I want to get help."

"Tim promised to help. You can't stop him."

"I can and I will!"

Boon bent his face down to hers until their noses were almost touching. "Don't let your anger at me stop Tim from doing what's right."

Suddenly realizing it was useless to argue, Kayla bit back further angry words. Could Boon be right about her feelings?

"I don't understand why you're so dead set against Tim helping the orphans," said Boon.

Shame suddenly washed over Kayla, and she turned her back on Boon. "Father God, forgive me," she whispered weakly. "I'm that sorry for being such a shrew." Tears burned her eyes. Slowly the anger seeped away. "Father in Heaven, You're my strength and my help. You guide my path . . . And Timothy's. With You with me I'm willing to help the orphans to safety."

Just then Kayla heard the rattle of the wagon and Timothy calling to the mules. She turned to see him backing the wagon through the wide doorway of the livery. He stopped with the wagon inside, the mules standing at the doorway.

Timothy jumped down, his face alight with excitement. "Boon, bring them out . . . Quickly! Deems was inside the general store."

Kayla ran to Timothy. "I'm that sorry, Timothy! Forgive me. I'll help all I can."

Timothy grinned at her. "Thank you. I thought you would."

Her dark skirt flapping about her thin legs, Marigold stepped up to Timothy. "I don't trust her! She'll get us caught for sure."

Kayla shook her head. "I won't."

"She'll help," said Timothy.

"I still don't trust her," muttered Marigold as Beryl walked to her side, her eyes wide with fear.

Abb ran to the door and cautiously peered out. "No one's in sight. We gotta go now!"

Boon pitched a tarp into the back of the wagon. "Hide under that until you're out of town."

"Hurry," said Timothy.

Beryl tied her heavy bonnet in place, hesitated, then climbed into the wagon and crept under the tarp.

Marigold sighed heavily. "Won't we ever be safe again?"

Kayla's heart went out to her, but she didn't say anything. She knew it would take a while for Marigold to trust her. Silently Kayla prayed for all of them as Marigold and Abb slipped under the tarp.

Just then the small black boy Kayla had seen hiding behind the rain barrel jumped out of a stall. "Y'all please take me too," he said, his voice quivering.

"Leroy!" hissed Abb. "I thought you got away."

"I 'most did," said Leroy, shivering. His dark eyes looked huge in his small, pinched face.

"Quick, get in," said Timothy.

Leroy scrambled in and crawled under the tarp.

Kayla bit her lip to hold back her objections. Where would they ever find a home for these kids? From deep inside she heard, "With God all things are possible." She smiled, lifted her chin, and ran to climb up on the high front seat of the wagon. Yes, with God all things were indeed possible!

"Good-bye, Kayla," said Boon.

She looked over her shoulder and even managed to smile. "Good-bye, Boon Russell."

"Be careful, Tim," said Boon.

"That I will!" Timothy laughed and slapped the reins against the backs of the mules.

Kayla braced her feet as the wagon swayed and rolled out of the livery and onto the narrow frozen dirt street.

Icy wind whipped against them as Timothy drove past the Petre place and out into the wide, open prairie. Tall ice-coated grass swayed in the wind. Timothy's hands felt numb with cold, even through his gloves as he gripped the reins. He'd tied a scarf over the top of his wide-brimmed hat and down under his chin, but still his ears felt cold.

Kayla huddled into her ugly brown coat, glad for its warmth. She moved closer to Timothy and spread the horse-hair lap robe over his legs, then hers. "I'm sorry I was cross with you, Timothy."

He grinned mischievously. "'Twas Boon you were upset with, but you took it out on me and the orphans."

Kayla flushed and nodded. "You're right as rain, Timothy O'Brian. When did you get so smart?"

"I was born that way!" Timothy laughed.

Kayla smiled, glad to see he'd forgotten about his size for a while. She turned to tell the others it was safe to come out from under the tarp when she saw a man on horseback racing toward them. "Someone's coming, Timothy," she said sharply.

He looked back, then leaned forward and slapped the reins down hard on the mules as he yelled, "It looks like Deems!"

"It's hard to see," said Kayla, swaying back and forth. "But in town Deems was driving a wagon."

"With a horse tied on back . . . A black one, just like the one pursuing us now."

Kayla knew at the speed the horse was coming Deems would catch them soon. What would happen if he found the orphans in their wagon? Would he kidnap the O'Brians too and send Kayla to Ogallala to work in a saloon and Timothy to the workhouse in Kansas?

Just then they rounded a hill, and Timothy pulled the mules up short. He turned and jerked off the tarp. The orphans looked frightened. Beryl was crying against

Marigold's arm. "Jump out and run around the hill out of sight. Hurry! We'll come back for you after Deems leaves."

Kayla's stomach knotted as she watched the four kids jump to the ground and run away. Leroy fell, and Abb lifted him up and held his hand as they ran. Kayla pulled the tarp in a heap over Pansy's supplies, then held on tight as Timothy shouted to the mules.

The wagon creaked and bumped and swayed, sending Kayla almost flying out. Silently she thanked God for sending His angels to protect them and the kids.

Just then a shot rang out. Timothy gasped, and Kayla's blood ran cold. She glanced back to see Deems almost on them, a smoking gun aimed in the air.

"Stop!" Deems shouted, shooting in the air again.

"Please stop, Timothy!" cried Kayla. "He might try to shoot us if you don't."

Timothy pulled back on the reins. His arms felt as if they were being pulled from his shoulder sockets, but finally he stopped the team of mules. Shivers colder than the constant Nebraska wind ran up and down his spine as Deems stopped beside them. Sparks flew from Deems's blue eyes. The nostrils of his wide nose flared. His leathery face was red with cold.

Kayla gripped the lap robe and held it to her. Her mouth felt cotton-dry. "Why is it you stopped us, sir?" she asked sharply.

The big black stallion reared, and Deems pulled him into submission. "I want a look in the back of your wagon," snapped Deems.

"You have no right," said Timothy, sounding very brave, though he was trembling inside.

Deems waved his pistol. "This gives me the right." He

dropped to the ground, then climbed up on the side of the wagon and jerked the tarp back, uncovering Pansy's supplies. Muttering angrily Deems dropped to the ground, then mounted his snorting black stallion. "I'll find them kids if it's the last thing I do."

Timothy wanted to tell him he'd never find them, but he kept the words back. He knew better than to anger Deems worse.

Kayla looked down her nose at Deems and said, "Have a merry Christmas next week. And the orphans too."

Deems cursed roundly, turned, and galloped away. The sudden silence made Kayla nervous.

Finally Timothy turned the wagon and drove back the way they'd come. Deems was a black dot on the road ahead of them.

Kayla sat stiffly beside Timothy as he reined in where they'd dropped off the kids.

"We're back," called Timothy. "Abb! Girls! Leroy!"

Kayla frowned slightly as she watched for them to run around the hill to the wagon. "Where are they?"

"You're safe!" called Timothy. Had they been eaten by a wolf or a coyote? "Come on, kids!"

"Deems has gone on his way," called Kayla. "Come get in the wagon before you freeze."

Finally Abb walked into sight, then waved for the others to join him. "It's safe," he called.

They raced to the wagon and scrambled in, shivering with cold. Leroy looked ready to drop in his tracks, but Abb helped him.

"Sit up close to the front of the wagon and wrap the tarp around you to keep the chill out," said Kayla.

"We'll sit where we want," snapped Marigold.

"Don't be mean, Marigold," said Beryl weakly.

Marigold scowled at her, and Beryl ducked her head.

Kayla shrugged and turned back. She looked down the road toward the turnoff. The prairie stretched on and on like the ocean had when they'd sailed to America. "It's getting late. We'd better hurry, Timothy. Pansy will be that worried about us."

Timothy nodded as he urged the mules forward with a call and a flick of the reins.

Kayla slid close to Timothy and once again shared the lap robe with him. "What will Pansy say when we drive in with more than her supplies?" whispered Kayla.

"She might surprise us and be glad to help," said Timothy.

Kayla bit her lip. "'Twould take a miracle, Timothy."

"I know," he said softly.

Kayla suddenly laughed. "But, Timothy, God is in the miracle business!"

Timothy nodded. "That He is!"

Kayla glanced back at the kids. They looked cold and frightened. Even Abb had lost the sparkle in his eyes. Fear pricked Kayla's skin, but she shook her head. She dare not allow fear to overtake her and drive away her trust in God!

The Christmas Tree

Kayla ducked her head against the icy Nebraska wind. The sky seemed even darker, and she wondered if they'd be caught in a blizzard. She thought about the time at Pansy's when a blizzard had struck so hard she couldn't see the house from the barn. She'd followed the sound of Pansy's bell and so made it to the house. Jane had told her about a man who'd missed his house and wandered off into the prairie, then froze harder than a buffalo chip. They hadn't found him until spring.

Shivering, Kayla glanced at the sky, then looked off across the prairie. Suddenly she spotted a spindly cedar tree near Bitter Creek. All thoughts of blizzards and frozen men left her head. Laughing excitedly, she turned to Timothy. "Stop so we can get that grand tree, Timothy!"

He looked to where she was excitedly pointing. The

tree was less than three feet tall with only a few branches and had green and rusty-brown needles. "It's not much of a tree."

"But 'tis no other!"

Timothy looked around at the wide sweep of prairie and finally nodded. The only other trees were the two tall cottonwoods farther down the creek. He turned the mules off the trail and drove to the tiny tree. "We're going to cut a Christmas tree!" he shouted, then laughed at the sound of his voice in the vast silence of the open countryside.

"Don't stop!" cried Marigold, plucking at the back of Timothy's coat. "Deems might still be after us!"

"We would've seen him," said Kayla.

"How do you know?" snapped Marigold.

"Just look around you. Where would he hide?" asked Kayla.

"Do you always get what you want?" Marigold scowled at Kayla while Beryl trembled beside her.

Kayla shrugged and smiled. She would not give a sharp answer. "We want the tree for the family," said Kayla. "It's important."

Angrily Marigold turned away. She whispered something to Beryl, then was silent.

"We're safe now or I wouldn't stop," said Timothy.

Leroy jumped up and leaned against the seat. "I never seen no Christmas tree just growin' like that."

"We have to saw it down and take it home to decorate it," said Kayla. She motioned to the tool chest. "Open that and hand me the saw."

"I'll cut it," said Timothy as he took the saw and jumped to the ground. His hands were so numb with cold, it was hard to hold the small saw. He leaned over the tree and sawed the trunk as low to the ground as he could. He liked the smell of the cedar. The tree toppled over, and he gingerly picked it up. The sharp needles stabbed him through his gloves as he carried it to the wagon. Weeds and snow clung to the tree, and he tried to shake them off but couldn't.

"That's sure an ugly tree," said Abb as Timothy laid it in the back of the wagon.

Kayla laughed. "'Tis the only tree for miles around, so it's beautiful to us. Pansy said she decorated a tumbleweed one time. Our tree is better than a tumbleweed."

Timothy laughed as he climbed back in place and drove the mules back to the trail.

When Timothy almost reached the trees that blocked the north wind from Pansy's house, Kayla turned and said, "Hide under the tarp again until we see if Pansy will let you stay."

Kayla watched as the orphans crawled under the tarp. She and Timothy had to find a safe place for them to live!

With a quick look at Kayla, Timothy stopped the mules near the front porch. "Stop worrying, Kayla. 'Tis the Christmas season . . . The time to be full of love."

"But do the people around here know that, Timothy?"

"We'll help them learn it." Timothy looped the reins around the brake handle, but before he could jump down Pansy and Czar stepped out of the house.

"What took you so long?" snapped Pansy with a frown. Her long coat flapped back to show the gun and holster around her wide hips. A hat covered her thin gray hair. "I been beside myself the last hour."

Czar sniffed the wagon and growled. Kayla's heart thudded so hard she was sure Pansy could hear. "We ran into a bit of trouble," said Kayla as she dropped to the ground. Her toes tingled with cold.

"I can tell by the sound of your voice you been up to something," said Pansy as she tried to peer in the back of the wagon. She was too short to see in from the ground, and her eyes were too bad to see from the porch.

Suddenly Leroy sneezed, then sneezed again. "Kayla O'Brian, who's hiding back there?" cried Pansy in her raspy voice. Czar growled louder, his nose almost touching the wagon bed.

Kayla darted a startled look at Timothy, and he stepped up to Pansy with a chuckle.

"'Tis no one to fear. We found someone who needs help," said Timothy. "Show yourself, Leroy."

Leroy peeked out from under the tarp, then slowly stood, his eyes wide with fright. "Don't let that dog of yours bite my head off," said Leroy, shivering inside his tattered coat. "I'm not good to eat."

Pansy stared at Leroy. "That's a Negro boy! Is he a runaway slave?"

"Pansy, the War between the States has been over a while," said Kayla. "There aren't slaves any longer."

"You should tell all them folks I worked for," said Leroy, rolling his eyes. "They said I was a slave and always would be."

"They were wrong," said Timothy, helping Leroy to the ground.

Leroy backed away from Czar. "Don't let that dog bite my head off!"

Kayla stepped closer to Leroy and slipped her arm around his shoulder. "Czar won't hurt you."

"Don't count on it," said Pansy grimly. Leroy shivered, and Kayla patted his arm. "If you kids don't beat all," said Pansy, shaking her head as she continued to stare at Leroy.

Timothy lifted Pansy's supplies from the wagon and carried them inside while he tried to think of a way to tell Pansy about the other kids.

Just then Czar looked up and barked.

"Somebody's coming," said Pansy, flipping back her long coat and resting her hand on her gun handle.

Kayla looked in the direction Czar was looking, and she finally made out the big black stallion. Her blood froze in her veins. "It's Deems!" she cried in alarm. She turned to Pansy. "That man's after the orphans to do bad things to them. Please help them!"

"What orphans?" asked Pansy sharply.

Czar barked.

Just then the girls and Abb jumped from the wagon and huddled on the porch behind Kayla and Leroy. Pansy stared at them in shock, and Czar growled.

"They need help, Pansy," said Kayla.

Timothy walked out the door and stepped up to Pansy. She was shorter than he was. "Please don't let that man know the kids are here. He's bad! Where can the kids hide?"

"In the spare bedroom," said Pansy crisply. "Get them in there fast, and then you get right back out here."

"I'll take them," said Kayla. She knew her way around Pansy's place better than Timothy did. She ran to the door with the others following.

"You better have a good story to tell me later," said Pansy in a low, tight voice.

"We do," said Timothy. "Just help us keep them from Deems."

Pansy pulled her gun and kept her hand on Czar's head. "He won't get them kids if I can help it!"

Inside the spare room Kayla looked around. "Two of you hide in the wardrobe and two of you under the bed," she said. "And don't make a sound."

Marigold narrowed her eyes. "How do we know we can trust you or that old lady?"

"Hide quickly just in case Deems forces his way past Pansy! We can talk about trust later." Kayla ran back outdoors and waited on the porch with Pansy and Timothy.

"You kids got a lot of explaining to do," said Pansy gruffly as she peered toward Deems. He was too far away to hear them.

"We'll tell you all about it after we get rid of Deems," said Kayla. Silently she prayed for protection.

Pansy shook her head. "I lived the past several years without seeing a soul for days at a time. Since you two came, this has become a regular stagecoach stop. I don't like it a bit!"

Kayla stepped closer to Timothy and waited for Deems. She could tell the man looked very angry. Why had he come after them again?

When Deems was several feet away Pansy called, "Stop right there, stranger! State your business."

"I came to get my kids. These two helped them run away." Deems waved his gloved hand toward Kayla and Timothy. "They tricked me before, but I suspicioned they was guilty, so I checked around and I seen where my kids hid in the snow. I came to get them."

"They aren't his kids," whispered Kayla. "Don't believe him, Pansy."

"You hightail it out of here, stranger!" cried Pansy. "I won't let you badger my grandkids."

Kayla and Timothy looked at each other in surprise. Pansy had called them her grandkids!

Deems pulled off his hat, rubbed his hair, then dropped his hat back in place. "I want them to tell me where my kids are! It's against the law to keep them from me."

Timothy bit his tongue to keep back angry words that would've given too much away. He had to keep calm so Deems would ride away. Timothy's temper seemed like a live thing inside him, fighting to get out.

Kayla felt the tension as she continued to silently pray for protection. She watched Deems reach for his rifle. Would he try to shoot them in their tracks?

Suddenly Pansy shot, and the sound rang across the silent prairie with a report that almost deafened Kayla. Her ears rang.

Deems lifted his hands, the reins still clasped in one of them. "Don't shoot! I don't mean you no harm."

"Get off my place right now!" Pansy sounded as if she'd shoot if he didn't.

Kayla trembled as she remembered the first time she'd seen Pansy. Pansy had held a rifle on her until she'd learned Kayla could read and write. Pansy especially liked Kayla to read about Russia, where her father had lived before coming to America. Kayla knew nothing Deems could say would make Pansy lower her gun. He probably didn't know how to read, nor would he know anything about Pansy's precious Russia.

"I mean to get them orphans back, no matter what it

takes!" shouted Deems as his black stallion reared, pawing the air, then dropped back to the snow-covered ground.

"Not if I can help it," muttered Pansy.

Kayla heard and smiled. With Pansy helping them, the orphans would be safe.

Finally Deems whirled his stallion and galloped away.

Czar whined and rubbed his neck against Pansy's skirt.

"I recall seeing a Negro man north of here," said Pansy with her eyes still on Deems. "Rides a big white stallion. Giant of a man." Pansy nodded thoughtfully. "He had to have a special-built saddle for him and his horse."

"Maybe he'd want Leroy," said Timothy.

"And maybe not," snapped Pansy. "You kids got us in a heap of trouble. I don't know what Rachel's gonna say about this."

"Could the kids stay with you?" asked Kayla.

Pansy pushed her hat back on her head and narrowed her blue eyes. "Them two girls looked about as useless as a sandstorm in the summer, but them boys might be of help."

"Thank you, Pansy!" cried Kayla.

"You have a heart of gold!" said Timothy.

Pansy scowled. "Don't go getting any ideas! I'll help get that Leroy boy to the Negro man up north. We'll see about the other boy."

"Do you know anyone who'd take the girls?" asked Kayla.

Pansy shook her head. "It won't be Rachel, I can tell you that right now."

"She might surprise us," said Timothy as if he knew something they didn't know. He often knew things ahead of time, the way Mama had.

Kayla suddenly realized how hard it would be to share the Larsen family with Marigold with all her prickles and sharp tongue, and with frightened, timid Beryl too.

Kayla's heart sank. Then from deep inside she heard, "You can do all things through Christ who strengthens you." She lifted her chin, squared her shoulders, and walked to Pansy's spare room to get the orphans.

Home Again

Inside Pansy's kitchen Kayla called, "You kids can come out now."

"And don't steal anything of mine!" shouted Pansy as Czar stood guard beside her.

Heat from the kitchen range seeped deep inside Kayla's bones, and she didn't want to think about the biting cold they would face on their last mile home. She glanced out the window as Timothy watered the mules. He looked cold, but she knew he wouldn't have time to get warm before they headed for Bitter Creek Ranch. The wind had risen, and the sky had darkened.

Abb walked into the kitchen with Leroy directly behind him and the girls in back of Leroy. "Is Deems gone?" asked Abb with a quick frightened look around.

"Yes," said Kayla. "Pansy scared him off." Kayla smiled proudly at Pansy. "This is Pansy Butler." Kayla explained who Pansy was, then introduced the orphans. "Pansy said she'd help you. Abb and Leroy, she'll keep you here with her. You girls will go with us. I'm sure the Larsens will help you find a good home."

"Don't count on it," said Pansy under her breath, but the girls heard.

"What do you mean?" asked Marigold sharply.

"Wait and see," said Pansy as she lifted the lid on the stove and poked a chunk of wood in. Sparks flew, and smoke drifted out before she dropped the lid in place with a clatter.

"Will they give us back to Deems?" asked Beryl with a shiver.

"They won't do that," said Pansy. "I don't think they will."

Marigold turned to Kayla. "You better not make more trouble for me and my sister."

"I wouldn't do that," said Kayla.

"I don't trust you," said Marigold.

"It looks like you'll have to," said Pansy.

"I want to go with Timothy," said Abb as he flipped his shaggy brown hair out of his eyes.

"You can't always get what you want in this life," said Pansy. "I found that."

Abb looked at Pansy as if he were afraid of her. That seemed funny to Kayla since Abb looked like a giant next to Pansy. "What would I do here?" he asked.

"Help with chores for one thing," said Pansy. "You're a big boy and should be able to do everything."

"I could stay here too," said Leroy as he carefully held his hand out to Czar. "I could feed and water your dog."

"You're going to that Negro man," said Pansy. "He'll be glad to have you, I would imagine."

"Nobody wants me," said Leroy.

"I want to go back to Ohio," said Beryl, standing as close to Marigold as she could get.

"We can't go back!" snapped Marigold.

Abb started for the door, but Kayla blocked his way. "I'm going with Timothy," he said gruffly.

Kayla knew he could walk right over her if he wanted to, but she didn't step aside. "Please stay here with Pansy. It'll make less trouble for us, and you'll be a big help to Pansy. It's hard for her to get out in the snow and cold to do the chores."

"I can do my chores by myself, Kayla O'Brian!" snapped Pansy. "Don't tell this boy I can't!"

Kayla grinned at Pansy. "If he were here to help, it would be easier for you, and you know it."

Pansy shook her finger at Kayla and Abb. "Get this straight! I don't *need* any help, but I could *use* some."

Kayla nodded. She knew Pansy's pride. "Abb, would you stay here a while at least? You could see Timothy often."

"Why can't I go with you now?" asked Abb.

"Because my daughter won't let you," said Pansy. "Rachel has her hands full, and she won't take in more kids."

"I guess it's better to stay here than to go to the work-house in Kansas," said Abb as he sank to a kitchen chair.

From outdoors Timothy called for them.

"We'll see you soon, boys," said Kayla. "Thank you, Pansy."

"I don't like fighting off Deems in my old age," said Pansy.

"You love every minute of it," said Kayla with a laugh. "You could teach Abb how to shoot."

Abb jumped up, and his eyes sparkled once again. "I'd like that!"

"Me too," said Leroy.

Pansy laughed. "You hear that, Czar. Already they got me doing things for them!"

Kayla led the girls to the wagon and climbed inside. "Hide under the tarp again just in case Deems is somewhere out there waiting for us."

Beryl moaned, but Marigold slipped under the tarp without a sound.

Timothy slapped the reins on the mules, and the animals walked away from the house and out into the prairie. Timothy wanted to get home to a big meal and a warm house. Suddenly he frowned. He wasn't looking forward to the looks Abel sometimes gave him that could easily mean Abel wanted to be rid of him because he was so small. How he hated standing beside Greene! He was sure everyone was comparing them. At the same time he did want to see if the three horses had been exercised, a job he usually did himself. Greene wasn't good with horses, and Abel's leg still wasn't very strong.

Kayla sighed as Timothy drove past the very spot where she'd found Boon Russell a few weeks back. She'd thought all her feelings for him were gone, but one glimpse of him in town and they'd come rushing back, even though she knew he preferred Clare. Kayla locked her hands together in her lap and watched a crow flying across the ever-darkening sky. She'd convinced herself that Boon was no good, but then he'd helped the orphans escape from Deems. Kayla shook her head. What was the true picture of Boon Russell? Would she ever know?

Up ahead Kayla saw the huge barn, the granary, the sheds, and the Bitter Creek Ranch house. A horse stood near the wrap-around porch of the house. As they drew nearer, Kayla gasped and gripped Timothy's arm. "Deems!" she hissed. "See his black stallion?"

Fear pricked Timothy's fingertips, and his stomach

tightened into a hard ball. "We'll have to make sure the girls stay hidden. Crawl back and tell them what's going on, but stay down. Anyone with good eyes could see this far away."

Kayla eased herself over the seat and down into the wagon bed.

"I'll slow way down, but I dare not stop in case Deems is watching," said Timothy. "Uncover the girls and throw the tarp over our Christmas tree."

Kayla lifted a corner of the tarp. She saw the sudden fear on the girls' faces. Marigold quickly masked hers, but Beryl didn't even try. "Deems is at the ranch. We're going to hide you girls in the shed. Stay there until someone comes for you."

The girls nodded, and for once Marigold didn't argue. Timothy drove the wagon up to the barn where he'd normally drive. It was out of sight of the house. "Jump out, girls! Hurry!"

Kayla jumped to the trampled snow, and the girls dropped down beside her. She led them to the shed, and they quickly slipped inside. She heard the kitchen door slam, and she raced back to the wagon to help Timothy unhitch the mules. Her heart raced as she listened for footsteps. She didn't turn at the crunch of snow under foot.

"It's about time you got back," snapped Rachel.

Kayla forced a smile as she turned. Rachel stood beside Deems, and they were both scowling. "We got the supplies for your mother, Rachel."

Timothy turned with a grin. "We brought you a grand surprise!"

Rachel frowned. "This man says you two helped his children run away."

"That we did not!" cried Kayla.

"From what I heard in town this man has no children," said Timothy. He almost laughed aloud at the anger on Deems's face.

Deems peered inside the wagon. "Ah ha! They're under the tarp!"

"Don't be touching our things!" cried Kayla.

Deems jerked up on the tarp, then scowled down in anger at the cedar tree.

"'Tis our Christmas tree," said Timothy.

A muscle jumped in Rachel's jaw. "A Christmas tree! What foolishness!"

"'Tis the only one we could find," said Kayla. "'Tis not a beauty, but once it's dressed in all its glory it'll be grand. We'll string popcorn and sew bright scraps of material into shapes."

Deems slammed his right fist into his left palm. His face was red, and he looked ready to burst. "Stop talking about trees when I want to know about the kids! Where are they? What did you do with them?"

"I'll put the mules in the corral, then check on the horses," said Timothy.

Kayla lifted the tree out and winced against the sharp prickles of the needles. "We'll set this up in the front room where we all can enjoy it."

Rachel narrowed her eyes as she watched Kayla and Timothy. "Answer the man," she said softly but firmly.

"He won't believe us," said Timothy.

"So why waste our words?" said Kayla.

Rachel chuckled. "It never seems to bother you to waste your words other times."

"We didn't take his kids," said Timothy over his shoulder as he led the mules to the gate.

"Timothy speaks the truth," said Kayla. "An O'Brian does not lie!"

Rachel turned to Deems. "That's true. They don't. We can't do more for you. You might as well ride back to town. Maybe they've turned up there."

Deems swore under his breath as he clenched and unclenched his fists. "I never give up. I'll get them kids back no matter what."

"Snow's coming," said Rachel as she pulled her long coat tighter around her thin body. "You'll have to hurry to make it back to town."

"I'd like to spend the night," Deems said.

Kayla's heart sank, but she didn't let it show. She knew Nebraska hospitality.

Rachel hesitated, but finally nodded. "You can bed down in the barn."

Kayla shot a look at Timothy, but he hadn't heard Rachel or Deems. She wanted to run to Timothy and tell him, but she didn't want Deems to be more suspicious than he already was. Kayla turned her back on Deems and Rachel and ignored the sharp stabs of the needles of the tree in her hand. How could she and Timothy get the girls inside without Deems seeing them?

Just then Timothy ran back to Kayla. "I'll carry the tree to the house." He felt her tension, and he looked at her questioningly. *What?* he mouthed.

"Deems is staying," she whispered.

Timothy caught his breath, and the ground seemed to spin like a top.

"Timothy, help Deems with his stallion," said Rachel.

Timothy turned and forced a smile at Deems. Timothy didn't want to do or say anything that would give away their secret. "You should be proud of your stallion. He's a grand piece of horseflesh."

Deems scowled at Timothy. "What do you know about horses?"

"My papa was the best trainer in all of Ireland," said Timothy as he walked toward the house with Deems.

Kayla's head spun. How could she get the girls into the house without Rachel or Deems seeing them?

The Christmas Angel

Kayla watched Rachel walk to the donkey pen, then glanced toward the barn as Deems and Timothy led the black stallion inside. Suddenly she had an idea. "Timothy, show Deems our horses," called Kayla. "He is a man who knows horses."

Deems scowled back at Kayla. "I'm not here to look at horses."

"We have three beauties," said Kayla. "Tell him, Timothy."

Timothy hesitated, then realized Kayla wanted him to keep Deems busy so she could sneak the girls inside. This was the perfect time. The others were busy with chores, and Abel probably was in the front room resting his leg. "You'll have to see the horses to believe them," said Timothy.

Kayla waited until they were inside. Then she ran to

the shed, the cedar tree still in her hand. "Girls, come on now," she whispered. "Hurry!"

The door opened, and Marigold peeked out. "Is he gone?"

"No, but he's in the barn with Timothy. This is your only chance." Kayla leaned the tree against the shed. She'd take it in later. "Hurry!"

"I'm too scared," said Beryl, trembling so much Kayla wasn't even sure the girl could walk.

Kayla gripped Beryl's thin arm and pulled her in front of Marigold. "Come on!" Kayla dashed across the yard with Beryl beside her and Marigold close behind. They slipped inside the warm kitchen, and then Kayla led the way to the closed-in steps. "Try to walk softly," she whispered. She led the way upstairs, shivering at each creak, and opened the heavy paneled door to the room she shared with Ula and Jane. It was a tidy, large room with two beds, a wardrobe, two dressers, and a free-standing looking glass. "Inside . . . quickly!"

"Beds," whispered Marigold with her hands clasped at her heart. "I haven't slept in a bed for weeks!"

Kayla didn't have the heart to tell her she couldn't sleep in one tonight either if Rachel was in one of her ornery streaks.

Beryl pulled off her tattered coat, draped it over the footboard, and sank to the bed. Her brown eyes filled with tears. "A real bed," she said with a catch in her voice. She pulled off her shoes and slipped under the covers without taking off her calico dress. "It is a bed," she whispered. "It's not a dream." She turned on her side, curled up, and closed her eyes. Her face looked as white as the pillowcase.

Kayla stared at her in surprise. "You'll have to hide until I can tell the family about you."

Beryl lifted her head and looked right at Kayla. "No! I won't move from here!"

Kayla gasped in surprise at the stubborn look on Beryl's face.

Marigold pulled off her shoes and coat and crawled into bed beside Beryl. "We'll sleep until you wake us up."

Kayla shrugged helplessly, nodded, and walked out, softly closing the door. She stood in the hall and listened to the creak of the house and smelled the wood smoke and coffee from the kitchen. Just what would Rachel do when she learned about the girls?

Taking a deep breath Kayla walked downstairs, hung her ugly brown coat on a hook near the back door, fixed the fire, then walked to the front room to tell Abel about the girls. Butterflies fluttered in Kayla's stomach as she stopped beside Abel in his rocking chair. He had the newspaper over his face, and his long legs were stretched out in front of him. "Abel, I'm that sorry to be waking you, but I must speak to you."

He groaned and pulled the paper off his face. "What's this I hear about you and Timothy helping Deems's kids run away?"

"They're not his children," said Kayla, her chest rising and falling in agitation. What if Abel wouldn't help? What if he insisted they give the kids back to Deems? "They are not his children!"

Abel frowned as he sat up straight and studied Kayla through narrowed eyes. "Then who are they?"

Kayla clasped her hands together and forced back the nervous flutters in her stomach. "They're orphans, and he's going to sell the girls to a saloon-keeper in Ogallala and send the boys to a workhouse in Kansas."

Abel whistled softly. "So you did help them!"

"And what would you have us be doing? Leave them to his mercy?" Kayla flipped back her mass of black hair. "That we could not do!"

"Where are they?" asked Abel tiredly, looking around as if he expected them to be hiding behind the potbelly stove, the sofa, or the other rocking chair.

"The boys are with Pansy, and the girls are upstairs."

"What?" cried Abel, almost coming out of his rocker. "Does Rachel know?"

Kayla shook her head. "I wanted you to know first. You are the head of the house."

Abel grinned and wagged his finger at Kayla. "Don't use that oily tongue on me, young lady! I am the head of the house, but Rachel has to know about the girls anyway. You know that."

Sighing, Kayla nodded. "I don't know if I'll have the courage to tell her."

Abel chuckled. "I might not either."

"I'll go fix supper and let you decide what to do," said Kayla with a mischievous grin.

"Sure. Leave it to me!" Abel awkwardly pushed himself up.

"She is your wife."

Abel brushed his hand across his hair. "She sure knows how to hold a grudge."

Kayla stopped at the doorway and looked back. "We brought home a Christmas tree."

"You don't say!"

"A spindly cedar."

Abel laughed. "It beats anything we've ever had."

"Didn't you ever have a tree?"

A sad look crossed Abel's face, then was gone. "Me and my first wife did, but when she died and I married Rachel, she wouldn't have one, so I didn't insist on it." Abel leaned heavily on his cane. "I remember we had a special angel for the top of the tree. I tucked it away in the attic, and I think it's still there."

Kayla's blue eyes lit up. "Where? Could you get it?"

Abel slapped his leg. "It's too hard for me to climb the ladder to the attic, but you could look. It's in a wooden box about this big." He measured about twelve inches with his hands. "It was inside a trunk up there."

"I'll look right now!" Kayla's cheeks flushed with excitement as she ran up the stairs to the ladder that led into the attic. Cobwebs brushed her face. Thanks to the dim light coming through the lone window, she spotted the trunk. She raised the lid and saw a quilt lying on top, which she carefully lifted in order to find the wooden box underneath. She put the quilt back in place, closed the trunk and quickly climbed back down the ladder, the box firmly in her hand.

A few minutes later she found Abel at the kitchen table and held the box out to him. "Here it is," she said softly.

He stared at it a long time. "I can't open it," he said with a catch in his voice.

"Shall I?"

Abel nodded.

Kayla set the box on the table and slowly lifted the lid. She pulled back a soft white cloth, then gasped. A beautiful china angel with a white robe, glistening white wings, and a golden halo lay there. It was built to stand on a treetop. "It takes my breath away," whispered Kayla.

"It is beautiful," said Abel just above a whisper. "I had forgotten." He touched the pale pink cheeks on the angel's white china face. "Nan bought it our first and only Christmas. She paid too much for it, and I got mad." Abel groaned. "How foolish of me!"

"Have the others seen it?" asked Kayla.

Abel shook his head. "Not even Greene." Kayla knew he'd been only a baby when his mother had died. "I want him to have it when he gets married."

"He'll be pleased to have something of his momma's."

Abel nodded. He sighed again. "Close it up, Kayla. Put it in my dresser drawer, and we'll get it out when we decorate the tree."

Kayla reluctantly covered the beautiful angel and carried it to Abel's dresser. Just as she walked back into the kitchen Timothy stepped inside with Deems at his heels. Cold air rushed in, and Timothy quickly closed the door. He looked questioningly at Kayla to see if the girls were safely inside, and she barely nodded.

"I thought you'd be gone by now, Deems," said Abel.

"Your missus said I could bed down in the barn since a storm's coming," said Deems, pulling off his hat and coat. He combed his fingers through his dark hair, standing the gray streak on end for a minute.

"Wash up and sit here," said Abel, motioning to the chair beside him. "I want the news from the outside world. How're the ranchers making out? Many cattle freeze yet? Any run out of hay?"

Kayla shut out the conversation as she fixed the fire

and walked to the pantry for potatoes. She glanced out the window to see giant snowflakes swirling through the air.

Abel turned from Deems and said, "Timothy, bring in the Christmas tree and set it up in the front room. You'll find a couple of boards and nails in the shed. Cross them like this and nail them together, then nail the tree on the boards."

Timothy nodded as he reached for his hat and coat again. He ran through the snow to the shed, glad Kayla had been able to get the girls inside. He found Rachel standing beside the tree just looking at it.

"Do you call that a tree?" she asked gruffly.

Timothy grinned. "It's not much, but it'll be a fine tree by the time we finish with it."

Rachel lifted her chin high. "I won't have it in the house."

"I'm sorry you feel like that," said Timothy. "Didn't you ever have Christmas when you were a kid?"

"Of course."

"Your kids would like to have one too."

Rachel threw up her hands. "There's no winning with an O'Brian! Take it in, but don't make a mess doing it."

Timothy smiled at Rachel. "We'll make it a fine Christmas, Rachel. You'll see."

Rachel brushed snowflakes off her cheek. "Do you really think so?" she asked bitterly.

Timothy narrowed his eyes. "What is it that hurt you so much, Rachel Larsen?"

She gasped, then whirled around and strode to the house, slamming the door after her.

After supper Kayla stood in the kitchen and looked at the others around the table. Only Rachel sat in the front room, reading her book. Kayla glanced toward Deems and was surprised to see him smiling as he looked at the tiny tree Timothy had set near the door until they could decorate it. Maybe Deems still had a heart under all that meanness.

While Abel and Deems talked about the economy, the weather, and what the President of the United States was doing right and wrong, Kayla sat beside Ula and Jane as they strung popcorn in the light of a kerosene lamp. Ula was eating as much as she strung.

In the light of another lamp Greene, Scott, and Timothy sat across the table stringing dried fruit that Rachel had agreed they could use. From time to time Greene glanced at Kayla and smiled at her. She smiled back. Timothy saw the looks pass between the two, and he frowned. He didn't want Kayla to love Greene more than she did him.

Kayla picked up a sewing basket, sewed two circles of red fabric together, and stuffed them with scraps of material. She sewed a piece of red ribbon on it and held it up. "Won't it look pretty hanging on the tree?"

"It will!" cried Ula, her face beaming.

Timothy only shrugged and Kayla looked questioningly at him. Sometimes she didn't understand Timothy at all.

Just then Rachel walked in. "It's time for bed. It's almost 9."

Kayla froze. She knew Abel hadn't had a chance to tell Rachel about the girls since Deems hadn't left the house since coming in just before supper.

Abel pushed himself up. "I think I'll have another piece of Kayla's apple pie while the kids clean up. Deems, you better get to the barn so you can have an early start in the morning."

Deems nodded. "I hate to go out in the cold."

Kayla locked her icy hands together. She knew Deems was hinting that he'd like to stay inside for the night.

"You'll have shelter in the barn," said Abel.

Kayla relaxed.

Deems slipped on his coat and hat. "Thanks for supper," he said.

Kayla was surprised to hear his thanks.

He opened the door, and icy wind and snow blew in. "It looks like a regular blizzard out there." No one said anything, so he stepped out and quickly closed the door.

"Why is it you didn't offer to let him sleep in here on the floor?" asked Rachel crisply.

"It's better for all of us for him to be out there," said Abel. He grinned at Rachel. "We got company."

Rachel frowned. "Who?"

Kayla moved close to Timothy and waited for Rachel's explosion.

"Two girls," said Abel. "Orphans these two got away from Deems."

Rachel threw up her hands. "I'll be!"

"He was going to sell them to a saloon in Ogallala," said Kayla. "You wouldn't want that, would you?"

"Don't put words in my mouth, Kayla O'Brian! Tomorrow when Deems leaves here, those girls will go with him!"

Kayla fell back a step, her eyes wide in shock. Did Rachel really mean what she'd said?

Snowed In

9

Standing as close to Timothy as she could get, Kayla waited for Abel to speak. He studied Rachel thoughtfully. The tension in the kitchen grew and grew until Kayla thought she'd shatter into bits. Giant tears filled Scott's eyes and rolled down his round cheeks. Ula slipped her hand into Kayla's and clung tightly to her. Greene turned his back on everyone and looked out the window into the dark night. Jane gripped the back of a chair and watched her parents with wide, frightened eyes.

"Rachel," said Abel softly, "we can't send the girls into such a cruel fate."

"We can't keep them here," said Rachel as if the subject were closed. She pushed her blonde hair away from her narrow face and fingered the top button of her wool dress. "We already have a house full."

Kayla wanted to beg Rachel to help, but she forced back the words. There was a time to keep silent, even if it was hard for her to do so. She knew it was just as hard for Timothy.

"We can help them find a good home," said Abel.

"They are nothing to us!" cried Rachel, knotting her fists at her sides. Her wool dress hung loose on her tall, lean, muscled body. She seemed to be stretched as tight as a violin string. The wood snapped in the stove, and she jerked as if she'd been shot.

"They are not going with Deems," said Abel firmly. "He'll leave in the morning without knowing the girls are here. After Christmas we'll find a home for them. That's final, Rachel."

A muscle jumped in Rachel's cheek. Without a word she strode to the front room and into her bedroom, slamming the door.

Kayla slipped her arm around Ula and held her close. Timothy held Scott tightly to his side. He felt the wild beat of Scott's heart, just like the heartbeat of the wild rabbit he'd caught a few weeks ago.

Abel stabbed his fingers through his hair. "Your ma will come around. Sometimes life gets her down."

Slowly Greene turned, his face haggard. "She wants to send me off too, just like them two girls."

Kayla gasped. For one minute Timothy wanted Greene sent away too, but then he hung his head in shame. 'Twas wrong to want Greene gone from his own home.

Abel limped slowly to Greene and rested his hand on Greene's arm. They were the same size, strong and muscled. "You are my son, Greene. Rachel cares for you."

"No, Pa." Greene sounded close to tears. "She might if I was more like Timothy, with a gift of gab and able to make her laugh."

Timothy stared at Greene in surprise. Could Greene be jealous of him? Why would a big strapping boy be envious of *him*? It was impossible!

Abel shook his head. "Greene, we're all different because God made us that way. Rachel does love us all. It's just hard for her to let us see it."

Greene rubbed an unsteady hand over his eyes. "She don't love me at all."

Kayla wanted to hold Greene just like she was holding Ula, but she didn't move. Tears stung her eyes.

"She don't love none of us," said Jane just above a whisper.

"She never hugs us," said Ula.

Abel sank weakly to a chair, his leg out in front of him.

"Kids, your ma does love you. She just can't show it. Her feelings have been locked inside her a long, long time. Last month she accepted Jesus as her Savior, and He's helping her to change. So be patient, can you?" Abel looked from one to the other, his look begging them to understand. Finally they nodded, and he sighed. "We'll pray for her. God works miracles. We all know that. He brought us a breath of fresh air." Abel smiled at Kayla. Then he smiled at Timothy. "And He brought us a fine horseman. He can sure help your ma."

Abel's words wrapped around Timothy's heart. Maybe he'd been wrong in thinking Abel wanted to send him away because he was too small.

Scott rubbed his face against Timothy's shirt, and Timothy felt the wetness of the boy's tears.

Abel cleared his throat. "Kids, this is a good time for all of us to pray together."

Pain stabbed Kayla's heart as she remembered all the times Mama and Papa had prayed together with her and Timothy. Aside from mealtimes this was the first time Abel had prayed. The Larsens had not been praying people before the O'Brians had come.

Trembling, Jane eased into her chair.

Abel bowed his head, cleared his throat, and said, "Heavenly Father, we come to You in Jesus' name, asking You to help us be patient with Ma. Help us to show her we love her and help her to love us. And protect the orphans Kayla and Timothy brought us. Help them to find a good home where they'll be safe and happy. Thank You for hearing us when we pray and for answering us. You work miracles, and we thank You for it."

While Abel prayed aloud, Kayla prayed silently. She knew the power of the prayer of agreement—that when two or three agreed together, God would answer. She'd seen it happen many times.

Several minutes later Abel said good night to all of them. "Sleep well, knowing the answer's on the way," said Abel, smiling.

"That it is!" said Timothy, nodding.

"Yes," whispered Kayla. She carried the lamp to light the way up the narrow stairs. The others followed quietly.

At their bedroom Kayla whispered good night to the boys, then walked into the girls' room behind Jane and Ula. The room was chilly and smelled like kerosene. She held the lamp high, and it cast a soft light over the bed where Marigold and Beryl slept soundly. "Jane and Ula, you take the other bed, and I'll sleep on the floor," Kayla whispered.

Ula clung to Kayla's hand. "You can sleep with us."

"There's room," said Jane.

"Please," said Ula, her eyes big in her pale face.

Kayla finally nodded and kissed Ula's cheek. Kayla set the lamp on the dresser. She quickly undressed and slipped on her new nightdress she had sewed just last week. She braided her long black hair and helped Ula braid her brown hair. Kayla was too tired to write in her diary, and she didn't want to leave the light burning any longer than necessary in case it woke up the girls. Mama's diary was tucked in the back of Kayla's drawer, and she'd started writing in it the month before. It helped her sort out her feelings for Boon and for Greene, and even for Rachel.

Kayla watched Jane and Ula slip under the covers, then she blew out the lamp and slid in beside Ula. The sheet was cold, but the three of them together quickly warmed the bed. Her mind whirled with all the happenings of the day, but finally she drifted off to sleep.

When she woke the room was dark, but she knew it was already morning and time to dress. She fumbled in the dark for her clothes, shivering in the cold room.

Downstairs Kayla lit a lamp and quickly started the fire. She heard movement from Rachel and Abel's room and knew they were dressing. The rule was, whoever woke up first would start the fire. Usually it was Rachel.

Kayla huddled over the stove, warming her hands. She looked out the window just at daylight and gasped at the white world. Drifts higher than her head stood in some places, while other places were about knee deep. They were snowed in!

Just then Timothy ran into the kitchen and right to the stove, shivering with cold. "'Tis bitter!"

"And we're snowed in!" cried Kayla. "Snow, Timothy! Snow everywhere!"

He peered out the window. "Not even Deems will be able to leave here today!"

Kayla gasped. "What if he sees the girls?"

Rachel walked into the kitchen, pinning her hair in a bun. She glanced at Timothy and Kayla, then quickly away.

"Top of the morning, Rachel Larsen!" said Timothy gaily. "'Tis a winter wonderland outside."

"Good morning, Rachel," said Kayla brightly. "I hope you slept well."

Rachel scowled at them. "How can you two be so happy this early in the morning, and on such a cold, miserable day?"

"'Tis almost Christmas!" cried Timothy. "Today we decorate the tree."

Without answering Rachel filled the coffeepot with water from the pail and added the grounds. The smell drifted through the room. She set it on to boil, then stood with her back to the stove, warming herself.

"Deems won't be able to leave today because of the snow," said Kayla. "How will we keep him from learning about the girls?"

Rachel shrugged. "That's your problem."

Kayla's face fell, and she turned away. Why couldn't Rachel be more like Mama had been? But Kayla knew the answer to that. Mama had been a Christian most of her life, and she'd been happy. She'd loved Papa, and he'd loved her. Rachel had married Abel because his wife had died, leaving him with baby Greene. Rachel's parents had been afraid she'd run away with a worthless cowboy she was in love with and they'd forced her to marry Abel. She hadn't realized until just lately that she loved him and that he loved her. Someday Rachel would be a gentle, loving woman on the outside just as she was deep in her heart. But Kayla wondered if she'd have the patience to wait for that time to come.

Just then Kayla heard footsteps on the porch. Timothy opened the door, and Deems walked in, shivering with cold.

Deems lifted his hat. "Morning, all. Could I trouble you for a cup of hot coffee?" he asked Rachel with a smile as he stood over the stove, his face red and his boots covered with snow.

Rachel poured a cup of steaming coffee and handed it to Deems.

"I'll milk the cows when I warm up," he said. "I want to pay for my keep. It looks like I'll be here for a while."

Just then the kids ran down the stairs and burst into the kitchen, Greene and Scott first, then Marigold and Beryl with Jane and Ula. They stopped short when they saw Deems.

Kayla held her breath and stared from Deems to the girls and back again.

Timothy tried to think of something to do or say, but he couldn't make his brain respond.

Deems stared at the girls, and his face darkened with anger. Marigold gasped, and Beryl burst into tears. Kayla sagged weakly against the wall. What would happen now?

"You can't take the girls," said Greene in a voice much like his pa's.

Kayla bit back a surprised gasp at Greene's speaking up like that. He usually wouldn't talk in front of strangers, and he'd never showed such courage.

"They're mine, and I'll take them when I leave," said Deems grimly, his hand on the butt of his gun.

"Nobody's going anywhere," said Rachel sharply. "We're snowed in. Don't make more trouble, Deems."

"I won't make trouble," said Deems, picking up his cup of coffee. "But those girls will go with me when I leave."

"No!" cried Marigold.

"We won't," whispered Beryl, shaking her head hard. "And nobody will make us!"

Kayla watched Greene step back to the girls as if to protect them. Marigold smiled at him, and he smiled back, flushing painfully. Jealousy stabbed Kayla, and she abruptly turned away. Maybe Greene would never again look at her with the special love he had for her. He might reserve that look for Marigold.

Kayla bit her lip and tried to ignore another stab of that terrible jealousy.

Decorating the Tree

Kayla's fingers felt all thumbs as she buttoned her ugly brown coat, twisted her scarf around her head and neck, then pulled on her heavy work boots. Behind her, Abel talked with Marigold and Beryl as if they were part of the family. Ula and Jane were getting breakfast, and the others were outdoors doing chores. Kayla picked up the smelly chamber pots and stepped outdoors. The cold air slammed against her, hurting the inside of her nose. The snow muted Brownie's barking and Scotty's shouts. Greene had shoveled a path to the outhouse and the barn, so Kayla walked easily to the toilet to empty the pots.

"I wish we had left the orphans in Spade," muttered Kayla as she stepped outside the toilet and breathed the fresh crisp air. She heard Timothy's laughter, and she flushed with shame. What would he be thinking of her if he knew how she felt? And what was God thinking of her right at this minute? He knew her thoughts and feelings, even if no one else did. *An O'Brian was more than a conqueror through*

Jesus Christ! "Heavenly Father, forgive me. I'm that sorry for letting my feelings run wild. I will let Your love rule me."

Slowly Kayla walked back toward the house. A snowbank blocked her view to the west, but to the east the prairie stretched on and on like a huge white blanket. The pale blue sky reached down, down, down and sat on the white blanket like an upside-down bowl. It seemed as if the people of Bitter Creek Ranch were the only occupants of the whole world. Kayla shook her head. A mile away Pansy was probably out doing her chores, thankful Abb and Leroy were there to help her.

Just as Kayla reached the porch she heard Timothy call her. She turned and saw him on the path from the barn.

"Kayla, can you be coming to see the horses this morning?" Timothy shouted.

"That I can!" she called back as she set the pots on the porch. If she'd held on to her jealousy, she wouldn't have wanted to go near the barn in case she saw Greene. Laughing, she ran down the shoveled path and into the huge barn. A horse nickered, and George Washington, the donkey, brayed. Timothy stood at Big Red's stall with Deems beside him.

Timothy turned when he heard Kayla. "Deems here said he visited Buffalo Bill's ranch."

"And I saw the Wild West Show quite a few times," said Deems. He'd lost his anger and seemed excited.

Kayla had heard the Larsens talk about Buffalo Bill and knew he'd been a Pony Express rider, a scout for the army, and a guide for wagon trains.

Timothy looked ready to explode. "Deems said they're always looking for horse trainers!"

Kayla frowned. "Timothy, you wouldn't be leaving me here while you go train horses, would you?"

Timothy laughed and shook his head. "We could bring a few horses to Bitter Creek Ranch and train them right here! Deems says they pay top dollar."

Deems nodded. "Timothy told me how he picked these three horses out of a herd that stampeded through the ranch, and he told me about you two knowing horses. It's a good chance for you both."

"It does sound fine." Kayla couldn't believe her ears. What had happened to Deems? Why was he suddenly being so nice?

"I'll take Timothy to the ranch and introduce him to the head trainer," said Deems.

Kayla's stomach knotted, and a shiver ran down her spine. Was Deems offering to do that so he could kidnap Timothy? "We'll talk to Abel about it," said Kayla stiffly.

"He'll like the idea," said Timothy. "He'll want more horses here than mules, just like I do."

"You're right about that," said Kayla. She knew having the three top-grade horses had already brought back Abel's dream of having a horse ranch. Rachel had brought in the mules because she knew all about them. Abel had felt too defeated to stop her. The mules had made good money for them, but Abel knew horses would bring just as much, and he'd enjoy working with them.

"And we could make money on our own," said Timothy. "Someday we could buy a ranch and call it the O'Brian Ranch!"

Kayla smiled at Timothy's enthusiasm. It would be nice to have their own place when they were old enough.

Just then Jane shouted that breakfast was ready. Kayla

ran on ahead to take care of the empty chamber pots while the others followed. She heard Brownie bark and Scott shout with laughter. She glanced back and saw Greene. He smiled at her, and she smiled back. With a lighter step she walked into the kitchen to the noise of breakfast time.

Her face glowing, Ula ran to Kayla and grabbed her hand. "Pa says after breakfast we can all trim the Christmas tree!"

Kayla laughed happily. "I'm glad!"

Ula turned to Deems as he pulled off his coat. "Pa says you can help too if you want."

Deems looked surprised, then smiled. "I never helped trim a tree before."

"You can now!" cried Ula. She turned back to Kayla and whispered, "Pa says even Ma will help."

Kayla darted a look at Rachel. She was already seated at her place with a cup of coffee in her hand. She looked like she wanted to shout for silence, the silence that had filled the place before happiness had burst through.

In the middle of the morning Kayla crowded into the front room with the others as Greene stood the tiny tree on a table at the end of the sofa.

"String of popcorn first," said Abel from his rocking chair. He held a small wooden box on his lap, and only he and Kayla knew what was inside. "Jane, Ula, this is your part."

Jane blushed, but carried one end of the popcorn string while Ula carried the other. They wound it around the tiny tree, then stepped back to admire the white against the green boughs.

"A real beauty," said Timothy, grinning.

Rachel leaned back in her rocker and didn't say a word, but she looked at the tree with the rest of them.

"Dried fruit string next," said Abel, nodding to Scott.

Scott carried the string of dried apples to the tree, and Greene helped him wind it around, draping it nicely. Next Timothy helped Scott wind the dried apricot string around the tree.

"It does look like a real Christmas tree," said Beryl in awe.

"Now hang up the other things you made," said Abel.

Kayla hung the two cloth balls she'd sewed, while Marigold and Beryl hung other things.

"It's a beauty!" said Timothy, his blue eyes sparkling.

"Now for the surprise," said Abel, looking right at Rachel.

"Don't look at me!" she cried, gripping the arms of her rocker.

"Now for this," Abel said, holding up the box as he smiled at Rachel. "Rachel, you put the treetop decoration in place."

Rachel frowned.

"Do it, Ma!" cried the Larsen children.

Rachel jumped up. "Oh, all right!" She reached for the box, but Abel kept a firm grip on it.

"I'll take it out," he said softly.

Kayla hung back as the others pushed in close to see inside the box. She watched their expressions of awe as Abel lifted the lid and showed the angel.

"It's so beautiful!" The words seemed torn from Rachel against her will. She carefully took the angel from Abel and held it gingerly. "I've never seen such beauty."

Kayla saw Deems brush a tear from his eye as he cleared his throat.

"I had it tucked away in the attic," said Abel. "I knew it was time to take it out."

"It's prettier than anything I've ever seen," whispered Marigold.

Carefully Rachel set the angel in place on top of the tiny tree. She touched the glistening wings and the gold halo, then arranged the white gown. She stepped back beside Abel as one lone tear rolled down her sun-browned cheek.

"At the first Christmas, angels announced the birth of Jesus to the shepherds," said Abel softly. "This angel will help us remember Jesus is alive in Heaven today. Jesus loves us, and we love Him. He was born, He died, and He rose again for us." Abel's voice broke. "Thank You, Jesus."

"Thank You, Jesus," whispered Kayla. She glanced around the room and saw the others were as touched as she was. Even Deems was blinking away tears.

Kayla turned back to the tree to look at the angel. It was their very first Christmas without Mama and Papa. She glanced at Timothy and knew he was thinking the same thing. She wanted to run upstairs to hold Mama's diary and Bible, the only things she had left of the past, but she stayed in the front room with the others and looked at the tree.

Fun in the Snow

Kayla shielded her eyes against the glare of the sun on the snow to see where the boys were tunneling into a snowbank. The sun was bright, but not warm enough to melt the snow. Her toes tingled with cold as she ran toward Ula playing with Brownie.

"Kayla!" called Jane. "Want to make a snowman?"

Kayla nodded as she stopped beside Jane. She already had the body started.

"We're going to make a whole family," said Beryl, her eyes sparkling for the first time since Kayla had met her. "I'm making the ma, and Jane's making the pa."

"Then I'll make the child," said Kayla. She glanced around for Marigold. She was lying in the snow, making a snow angel by moving her arms and legs. Kayla turned back to the snow around her and started rolling a ball to make it into the base. Maybe Rachel would let her use a bonnet and a scarf.

Just then Marigold squealed. Kayla turned to see Greene chasing her through the snow. Jealousy stabbed Kayla, and she turned abruptly away. "I won't be jealous!"

she muttered as she patted the base of the snowman so hard she almost broke it apart.

"Boys always like Marigold," said Beryl. "They look right past me and fall in love with her." Beryl sighed heavily as she stood with one hand on her snowman. "I wonder if it'll always be that way."

"It won't be if you'll stop being so shy," said Jane.

In the distance Kayla heard sleigh bells. She lifted her head and listened, then spotted a team of mules coming, pulling a sleigh. "Pansy's coming!"

Beryl gasped. "Deems will see Abb and Leroy! He'll grab them and keep them again!"

"Abel won't let him," said Kayla.

"Grandma!" cried Ula, jumping up and down. "Wait'll she sees our Christmas tree!"

Kayla watched as the sleigh drew closer. She could see Abb was driving. Pansy sat beside him, with Leroy in the back of the two-seater sleigh and Czar next to him.

Abb stopped the mules near the barn, then jumped down and helped Pansy out. Pansy's face was flushed, and her eyes twinkled. She looked happier than Kayla had ever seen her. Maybe she'd let Abb stay on.

Timothy ran to Abb and said, "Deems is here!"

Abb fell back a step, his face ashen.

"He came looking for all of you and got snowed in," said Timothy.

"I'll be jiggered," said Pansy. "I hope Abel has him roped and tied."

"He's in the house talking," said Kayla. "But Abel said he won't let Deems take the kids."

"He's a slippery character," said Abb gruffly. "You can't

trust him. He can act smooth and nice, then turn on you and be mean. We better leave before he sees us."

"I won't let him take me," said Leroy, standing with Czar close at his side.

"We decorated the Christmas tree, Grandma," said Ula, smiling up at Pansy.

"Your ma let you do that?" asked Pansy in surprise.

"Pa did," said Jane. "But Ma put the Christmas angel on top of the tree."

"I brought some things over for Christmas," said Pansy. "That's why we came. Christmas is only a few days away. If you're going to have a tree, you might as well have some presents under it." She turned to Abb. "Get the bag out, and we'll take it to the house."

"I'm not going in the house where Deems can see me," said Abb, shaking his head.

"Greene will protect you," said Marigold, smiling at Greene as if she owned him.

Greene blushed.

Kayla wanted to push Marigold facedown in the snow, but she knew Jesus wouldn't want her to.

Abb looked at Greene as if measuring him in comparison with Deems. "Did you take the guns away from Deems?" Abb asked.

"No," said Timothy. "But we should."

"He hasn't acted bad," said Kayla. "Maybe he's given up on you kids."

"He hasn't," said Abb grimly. "I know him. Butter wouldn't melt in his mouth one minute and the next he's hotter than a blacksmith's forge."

Timothy glanced toward the barn. "I know where he keeps his rifle. He has his pistol on him."

"He keeps a gun strapped to his right leg," said Leroy. "I saw it one time when he didn't know I saw."

"I'll tell Abel," said Kayla. She wondered if he'd believe her after he'd spent so much time talking with Deems.

Pansy chuckled. "That man doesn't stand a chance against all of you." She patted the gun on her hip. "And me."

Kayla looked around at the orphans, the Larsens, and Pansy. They all had each other. Deems had no one. How sad. He was about Abel's age, but he'd said he had no family. She suddenly felt sorry for him. But that didn't mean she couldn't see his bad side. She knew faith in God could make a difference in his life. Silently she prayed for Deems. She knew the Bible said to overcome evil with good. Maybe they could even make a special Christmas gift for him.

Kayla glanced around at the others. None of them, except maybe Timothy, would agree to make a gift for Deems.

While the others talked, Kayla ran to the barn to find Timothy. He was hiding Deems's rifle behind a pile of hay in an empty stall. Quickly she told him her plan.

Timothy frowned, but finally nodded. "'Tis only right to do what the Scriptures say."

"Do you know what we could make for him?" asked Kayla.

Timothy slowly nodded. "That I do. His horse, Sill, is as important to him as Big Red, Roxie, and Offaly are to us. We could finish the fine halter we've been making for Offaly and give it to Deems for Sill."

The big black stallion nickered.

"He heard us speak his name," said Kayla with a laugh.

"He's a fine animal. Deems takes great care of him."
Timothy rubbed the stallion's face. "'Twould touch Deems to
the very heart for us to do something for Sill."

From the doorway Pansy said, "What're you two
cooking up?"

Kayla looked quickly at Timothy as he grinned at
Pansy.

"Should we be telling all our secrets now?" he asked,
standing with his feet apart and his fists resting lightly on his
hips.

Pansy chuckled. "It's that way, is it? Walk me to the
house for a strong cup of coffee before I head back home."

"What about Abb and Leroy?" asked Kayla.

"They won't step a foot inside with Deems here," said
Pansy. "They're even staying out of sight of the house."

"I'll go with you, Pansy," said Kayla.

"And I'll stay here with Abb and Leroy," said Timothy.

A few minutes later Kayla walked Pansy into the warm
house. The smell of coffee and baking pies filled the kitchen.
Rachel turned from the open oven door with a look of surprise on her face.

"Ma! I didn't know you were here!"

"Came in the sleigh," said Pansy as Kayla helped her
take off her coat. "And I brought some things for
Christmas."

"Not you too, Mama!" cried Rachel, throwing up her
hands.

Kayla listened to them talk as she hung up Pansy's
coat, then her own. She peeked in the front room where
Abel and Deems were hunched over a checkerboard, con-
centrating on the game.

Just then Marigold walked in, hung up her coat, and asked, "Is it all right if I go upstairs to rest?"

"Are you sick?" asked Rachel, frowning.

"Just a little tired," said Marigold, darting a look at Kayla. "I just need to rest a few minutes and I'll go right back out."

Rachel shrugged, and Marigold slipped quietly upstairs.

Kayla frowned thoughtfully. Just what was Marigold up to? She'd been laughing and playing happily just moments ago. Kayla excused herself and walked quietly upstairs. The bedroom door was partly ajar, and Kayla reached to push it open enough for her to walk through. But what she saw made her stop. Marigold had Kayla's drawer open, and she held Mama's diary in her hands! Kayla's heart dropped to her feet. The diary was open in the back where she'd been writing! Marigold was reading what she'd written a few days ago! Oh, it was too awful!

Abruptly Kayla pushed open the door and stepped inside. Red circles dotted her cheeks, and fire flashed from her blue eyes. She snatched the diary from Marigold and held it to her chest. "How dare you read my diary!"

Marigold flushed, but held her chin high. "If you don't want people to know your thoughts, then don't write them down!"

"This is personal and private!"

Marigold pointed at Kayla. "I knew you liked Greene! I knew you did! That's why you want to get rid of me. You know Greene really loves me and doesn't even notice you're around."

Kayla stared helplessly at Marigold. "What foolish talk!"

"It was the same with Boon Russell! You thought he liked me more than you, so you told him lies about me."

"What are you talking about? I didn't know anything about you. How could I tell Boon anything?"

Marigold paced the floor, wringing her hands. "You're glad Deems will make me be a saloon girl. Then no good man will want me for a wife. You think you're the only good girl around here. But you're wrong! I'm good, and I'll make a good wife for some man in another year or two. I could get married now if I wanted! I am fourteen, and lots of women out here get married that young."

Kayla shook her head. Marigold was acting like a crazy person. "What are you afraid of, Marigold?" asked Kayla sharply. "You're not going with Deems. He can't make you be a saloon girl. You don't have to get married until you are in love and want to get married."

Marigold dropped to the edge of the bed and burst into wild tears. "That's what you think!"

Kayla silently prayed for wisdom about what to say and do. "Marigold, what's wrong? Why are you so upset?"

"What do you care? You hate me!"

"I do not! I'm a Christian. With God's help, I love others with His love."

Marigold helplessly shook her head. "You can't love me. You can't! Nobody does!"

"Beryl does."

"She's my sister. She has to love me."

Kayla sat beside Marigold and folded her hands in her lap. The room was cold, and Kayla was beginning to feel the chill. "If you want to talk to me about what's bothering you, I'll listen and I promise I won't tell anyone."

Marigold shuddered. She picked at the quilt. "I have to

tell somebody!" She curled the tip of her braid around her finger. "Me and Beryl lived with our uncle in Ohio. The neighbor man's wife died, and Uncle made me marry the man."

Kayla bit back a gasp of surprise.

"Me and Beryl planned to run away before the wedding, but we couldn't make it, so we ran right afterwards. We got on a train and got off here in Nebraska. Deems found us just after we got off, and he said he'd find us a home. We believed him, but then we found out he was going to make us be saloon girls. So we ran away again, with Timothy's help."

The solution to this problem seemed impossible to Kayla, but she knew nothing was too hard for God.

"Now you'll probably make Abel send me back to Ohio, to that man Uncle forced me to marry."

Kayla shook her head. "You're fourteen! You shouldn't have to marry anyone yet!"

"Do you really mean it?" whispered Marigold, tears wetting her lashes.

"I mean it. But we should tell Abel and Rachel. They'll know what to do."

Marigold finally nodded. She licked her lips and smoothed her skirt over her knees. "Kayla, I'm real sorry about reading your diary."

"That's all right."

"I wanted to find something bad about you, so if you tried to make Greene stop liking me I could tell him the bad thing. I'm sorry."

"I write in my dairy to help me sort out my feelings. That's what Mama always did. I read her diary, and it helps me. But I read her Bible even more. It's my Bible now, and it's full of promises from God to help us."

"Is there a promise in it for me?"

"God says He will never leave you. He says He loves you. He promises to give you His strength and lead you in the path you should go if you'll follow Him."

"I never knew those promises belonged to me."

"They do."

Marigold gripped Kayla's hand tightly. "Promise me you won't let Deems take me."

"I promise."

"And that you won't let anyone send me back to that man."

"I promise."

Marigold sighed. "Thank you."

Kayla nodded. She'd just made some very bold promises, but with God's help she'd keep them. She stood up and smiled down at Marigold. "Shall we go finish building the snowmen?"

The
Unexpected
Visitor

Kayla stopped beside Rachel and looked in the pen at George Washington. Since yesterday, when Marigold had told her the terrible secret, Kayla had been trying to find a time to tell Abel. She'd found a brief moment to slip him the brooch, but then they were interrupted, and she'd walked away without telling him about Marigold. Now she knew Abel and Deems were once again huddled over a game of checkers. Deems must never learn the truth or he'd try to take Marigold back for any reward that might have been offered for her.

George Washington flicked his long ears and chewed a mouthful of hay. Brownie barked as he ran with Scott and Ula out into the prairie. The sun was still warm in the sky even though it was late afternoon. Much of the snow had melted. Deems had hinted he'd like to stay on for

Christmas, and Abel had invited him to do so. They talked horses and politics and played checkers. Abel didn't want to give that up during the long days of winter.

Rachel sighed heavily as she turned to Kayla. "Out with it, Kayla."

Kayla grinned. "You're learning to know me well."

"You bet I am!"

Kayla leaned against the top rail of the fence with her head and turned to Rachel. "'Tis a sad story."

"But one you'll tell me, no doubt," said Rachel drily.

"I must! 'Tis too much to hold back!" Kayla pushed back her mass of black hair, then told Rachel all that Marigold had said. "I didn't know how to help her."

"I do!" snapped Rachel, her eyes smoldering with rage. "Send her as far away from Ohio as she can get! Her uncle had no business forcing her to marry that man!"

Kayla knew Rachel was thinking of herself and her parents. "She's too young anyway," Kayla said softly.

"Yes, she is." Rachel pulled off her wide-brimmed hat and let the warm wind blow against her blonde head. "I'll help her find a good place to live. I don't know what to do about the man she was forced to marry. They *are* married, but Marigold could get an annulment. There's a lawyer in North Platte I could talk to about it."

"You've a kind heart, Rachel Larsen!"

Rachel scowled. "Tell me that when I won't let you have Christmas tomorrow."

Kayla grinned. "That's all talk, Rachel, and you know it. You want to see if you got a gift just as much as the rest of us."

Rachel strode away, then stopped and looked back at Kayla. "I don't want any presents! Not a one!"

"That's too bad," said Kayla with a giggle.

"Kayla O'Brian, what do you have up your sleeve?"

"Not me—Abel."

Rachel grew very still. "Is Abel going to give me something?"

Kayla nodded. "But a herd of wild horses couldn't be dragging it out of me."

Just then Timothy shouted, "A rider's coming!"

Kayla fell into step beside Rachel as they walked toward Timothy, Greene, Marigold, and Beryl waiting near the barn. A rooster crowed, and a duck quacked in agitation.

"It's Boon Russell," said Timothy in surprise.

Kayla's heart skipped a beat. Was it possible he was coming to see her?

Several minutes later Boon dismounted and left his horse standing with its reins dragging the ground. Boon looked ready to burst with news. He said hello all the way around, then smiled at Marigold and Beryl. "I hoped you girls were still here. I have news for you."

"What is it?" asked Marigold nervously.

"Deems is here," said Beryl.

"No!" cried Boon, looking around in alarm. "I wondered where he'd got to. He left his dog and his team of horses at the livery."

"What's the news?" asked Marigold impatiently as she plucked at Boon's coat sleeve. "Is it bad?"

"Deems won't like it a bit," said Boon, chuckling.

"Let's go in the barn and talk," said Rachel.

Boon nodded, and they all walked into the big barn and stood in a circle in the aisle between the stalls. The horses nickered out in the corral. Pigeons cooed in the rafters above. Boon pulled a newspaper from under his coat and slapped it against his palm.

"A man stopped by yesterday looking for you girls," Boon said.

Marigold gasped and stumbled to Greene, then gripped his arm as if she'd never let go. All the color drained from her face.

"What man?" asked Beryl, shivering.

"I won't go back," whispered Marigold. "I don't care what they do to me."

"You won't have to," said Rachel firmly. "I'll see to that."

Kayla smiled at Rachel, while Marigold stared at her with hope in her eyes.

Boon held up his hand. "Listen to me, Marigold. This is good news." His red hair looked bright in the dim barn, and his teeth flashed as he smiled. "The man said he was a friend to your uncle. When your uncle learned the man was coming west, he asked him to try to find you. He said he took a few days to look for you since he knew how important it was. I told him I knew where you were."

"Get on with the story," said Rachel impatiently.

Boon grinned. "The man said Noah Sandor is dead."

Marigold swayed and would've fallen, but Greene held her up.

"Who's Noah Sandor?" asked Timothy.

Kayla knew Noah Sandor was the man Marigold had been forced into marrying, but it was up to Marigold to tell the others.

"How do we know it's true?" asked Beryl sharply.

"It's in the newspaper. The man said you'd want proof,

and he left me the paper." Boon held it out to Beryl, and she glanced over it, then held it for Marigold to read.

"Then it's true," said Marigold as tears streamed down her cheeks. "I'm free!"

"What do you mean?" asked Greene.

"It doesn't matter," said Rachel.

"Here's a letter from your uncle," said Boon.

"What's going on here?" asked Timothy. He didn't like not knowing. He looked at Kayla, but he could see she wasn't going to tell him anything.

Marigold snatched the letter from Boon and tore it open, her hands trembling so hard she almost dropped it.

"What does it say?" said Beryl, trying to read over Marigold's shoulder.

Kayla's heart beat fast as she watched Marigold's face. "It must be good news," Kayla said.

Marigold looked up from the letter. She tried to speak, but couldn't. Finally she blurted out, "Noah Sandor signed the farm over to me on the wedding day. It's mine now . . . My farm."

"That's wonderful news," said Kayla.

Beryl tipped back her head and laughed. "Who would've ever thought this would happen! It's like one of those miracles you're always talking about, Kayla."

"It is," said Marigold.

"Now we can go back, Marigold!" cried Beryl. "We can go back and live on your farm! We don't have to run any longer."

Marigold nodded. "We can go right away." She smiled at Boon. "I just had a wonderful idea! You can go with us if you want. You can work on the farm."

Kayla suddenly felt weak all over. What would she do

if Boon wasn't close by for her to see from time to time? From the look on his face she knew he wasn't giving her a second thought. She bit her lip. When would she learn? Boon didn't care about her.

"Maybe Abb and Leroy will want to go with us too!" cried Beryl. "They need a home."

Marigold turned to Kayla. "You can come too. You and Timothy! We'll raise horses if you want."

A tingle ran over Kayla as Marigold's excitement spread to her.

"Kayla and Timothy can't go with you," snapped Rachel, taking Kayla by surprise. "They belong here with us." Rachel frowned at Kayla, then Timothy. "You wouldn't want to leave us, would you?"

Kayla hadn't really thought about it. She'd never had a choice before. It was a heady thought.

"Our own horses, did you say?" asked Timothy.

Rachel gasped. "What would we do without the two of you? No! . . . You can't go!"

"I could," said Greene stiffly. "I'm a strong worker."

Rachel stared at Greene in shock. "But this is your home! What would your pa say?"

Greene shrugged. "What would *you* say, Ma?"

Rachel looked like she was at a loss for words. "I say you're needed here, and you can't go," she said weakly. "Why would you even think of it?"

Greene turned and walked out of the barn, his shoulders bent and his head down.

Kayla stood helplessly by. She knew Boon, Marigold, and Beryl felt as much at a loss as she did.

Timothy stepped close to Rachel's side and whispered,

"He thinks you don't care for him. Go after him and tell him you do."

"Of course I do," whispered Rachel, but she didn't make a move to follow Greene.

Kayla wanted to push her after Greene, but she knew Rachel had a stubborn streak and would do things in her own way and in her own time. But what if it was too late? Kayla bit her lower lip. She didn't want Greene to leave. The family wouldn't be complete without him. It had nothing to do with her special feelings for him; it had to do with *family*. "Don't go, Greene," she cried silently.

Deems

Her hands locked over her heart, Kayla watched Boon ride away toward town. She knew he'd be back tomorrow for Christmas dinner. Rachel had invited him, and he'd quickly agreed. After that he was going with Marigold and Beryl to Ohio to check out the farm.

"You aren't really in love with him," said Marigold from behind Kayla.

Her face beet-red, Kayla whirled around to find Marigold and Beryl watching her. "I didn't say I was."

"I'll never fall in love," said Beryl, wrinkling her nose.

"Me neither!" cried Kayla.

Marigold grinned sheepishly. "I read your diary, remember?"

"Oh . . ." Kayla walked slowly to the porch and sat down on the top step. Marigold and Beryl sat beside her. "I've never said I'm in love, but I do have a strong attraction to Boon," said Kayla, locking her hands in her lap over her ugly brown coat.

"And to Greene?" asked Marigold softly.

Kayla nodded, flushing again.

"I know a girl who falls in love with every boy that comes along," said Marigold.

"I hope I'm not that way!" said Kayla, her eyes wide.

"I'm sure not!" said Beryl.

Marigold fingered the button on her coat. "I am. You gave me a promise that will help us, Kayla."

"Which one?"

"That God will direct our path. That has to mean even in our love life!"

Kayla nodded. She'd never thought of that before. "You're right, Marigold."

"Rachel doesn't talk about falling in love. My ma did though. I was twelve when she died; Beryl was eleven. Ma said she'd enjoy seeing us fall in love, get married, and have children."

Beryl rolled her eyes.

"Mama always said I was too busy thinking about horses to think about falling in love. She was wrong," said Kayla.

"You and Timothy won't be going back to Ohio with us, will you?" asked Marigold.

Kayla shook her head. "It was exciting to think about for a few minutes, but we belong here. They need us . . . And we need them."

Just then Deems stepped around the corner of the wrap-around porch. He had a cruel look on his face under his wide-brimmed hat. "What's this about going to Ohio?"

Startled, Kayla jumped up, Marigold and Beryl with her. "We thought you were playing checkers with Abel."

"I beat him again. Don't change the subject." Deems

flipped back his coat and patted his gun butt. "Answer my question."

Kayla's legs suddenly felt too weak to hold her, but she locked her knees and stood before Deems as if she weren't afraid.

"Beryl and I are going back to Ohio," said Marigold in a weak voice. "We don't need to find another home."

Deems scowled. "I'll lose money if I don't take you to Ogallala."

Kayla looked at Deems in shock. "You already know they aren't going with you." She glanced at the door beside her. "Abel told you."

"That cripple can't stop me from doing what I want!" Deems pulled his gun and aimed it right at Marigold. "I'm taking you and your sister, and we're getting out of here right now."

"No!" cried Marigold.

Whimpering, Beryl clung to Marigold.

Fear pricked Kayla's skin. She tried to think of something to do, but her brain felt numb. She'd convinced herself that everything was going to be all right. She and Timothy had even finished the halter for the black stallion and were going to give it to Deems tomorrow. Now suddenly, he'd changed back to the evil man he'd been when she'd first seen him. Abb had warned them that Deems was like that, but she hadn't believed him.

"Saddle Offaly and Roxie," said Deems to Kayla, never taking his gun off Marigold.

"You can't take our mares!" cried Kayla as she glanced helplessly around. Where were the others when she needed help?

"Don't tell me what I can or can't do! Now get to the

barn and saddle the mares! They'll bring me a good price when I'm ready to sell them."

"We won't take a step!" snapped Marigold, standing firmly in place on the porch with Beryl tight against her. "Shoot us dead right here if you must, but we won't go with you."

"You'll go all right," said Deems grimly. "You think I hung around here for the good company?" He waved his gun. "Walk ahead of me to the barn . . . Now!"

"No," said Marigold, shaking her head. A red braid slipped down her shoulder, and she flipped it back.

Beryl pulled away from Marigold, squared her thin shoulders, and lifted her chin. Her face was as white as the partly melted snowman in the yard. "Go ahead and shoot us. Then what money will you get?"

Kayla looked at the girls in surprise and admiration. She glanced at Deems. His face was dark with rage, and she was afraid he would indeed shoot them on the spot. His gun was aimed at Marigold. Suddenly, without thinking of the consequences, Kayla lunged at Deems and struck him hard in the chest with her shoulder. He fell back, and the gun exploded almost in Kayla's ear. The bullet went wild over Marigold's head and out into the prairie. Kayla smelled the gunpowder and kept hearing the ring in her ears.

Before Deems could regain his footing Marigold and Beryl jumped him, pinning him down to the porch. Her heart pounding, Kayla pulled his gun from his hand and stood back from him.

Suddenly the door burst open and Abel stood there, leaning heavily on his cane, his gun in his other hand. "What's going on here?" he asked in alarm. "What're you girls doing to Deems?"

Rachel ran from the barn, her rifle in her hand. She stopped short and stared at the girls and Deems. "What happened?" she cried.

Before Kayla could answer, all the others swarmed up on the porch, everyone talking at once.

"Greene, tie Deems up so the girls can get off him," said Kayla.

Timothy caught Kayla's arm. "Are you all right?"

She smiled shakily. "He was trying to take the girls away. And he meant to steal Offaly and Roxie."

"No!" Timothy shook his head. "How could he be so bad?"

Just then Abel whistled loud and long for attention. When everyone was quiet and looking at him he said, "I want an explanation of what happened here. And don't all of you talk at once!"

Kayla started the story, then Marigold took it up, with a few interruptions from Beryl. When they finished, everyone stared in silence at Deems.

Abel leaned heavier on his cane. "I'm sure sorry to hear this."

"They're lying," snapped Deems.

"They wouldn't lie," said Rachel.

"We do believe them," said Abel. "But now we have a decision to make about Christmas."

"This is not the time to talk about Christmas," said Rachel, frowning at Abel.

"Yes, it is," said Abel. "We agreed to let Deems stay for Christmas. Shall we let him stay, or shall we drive him into town to the sheriff right now?"

Deems stared at Abel as if he were crazy. "Don't play games with me, Larsen!"

"I'm not," said Abel. "I want to know what the family wants to do. Timothy and Kayla made a gift for you, and they have a right to give it to you if they still want to."

Deems grew very quiet. "Why would they do that?"

"Tell him, Kayla," said Abel.

"Because you don't have a family. You don't have anyone to give you a present," said Kayla.

Deems ducked his head.

"Send him to the sheriff now," said Greene. "He was going to shoot the girls."

"He was!" said Marigold. "I say let him spend Christmas in jail."

"Me too," said Beryl.

"What does Jesus want us to do?" asked Scott.

"Good question," said Abel.

Rachel pulled Scott close and kissed his round cheek.

Abel smiled at them. "Who says we let Deems stay? Raise your hand."

Kayla hesitated and looked at Timothy, and they both raised their hands. She looked around. Rachel and Scott raised their hands, and slowly the others did too. Greene was the only one with his hands at his sides.

"This is a cruel joke," said Deems.

"The vote stands, Deems," said Abel.

Rachel walked to Greene, put her hands on his shoulders, and looked deep in his eyes. "Greene, you're my son and I love you. Don't hold a grudge and lose out on the happiness you'll have by doing what is right."

A muscle jumped in Greene's neck, and then he slipped his arms around Rachel and hugged her tight.

A lump lodged in Kayla's throat.

Finally Greene stepped back from Rachel and raised his hand. "I vote to let Deems share Christmas with us."

Abel slapped Greene on the back. "I'm proud of you, son." Abel turned to Deems. "You are still welcome to have Christmas with us. What do you say?"

Deems swallowed hard and barely nodded. Kayla smiled through her tears.

Merry Christmas

Kayla took Pansy's coat and hung it on a hook by the door. It seemed like she'd been waiting forever for the time to gather in the front room for a Christmas celebration.

Abb stepped close to Timothy and whispered, "Are you sure Deems won't get free and kill us all?"

"He won't," said Timothy. "His ankles are shackled, but his hands are free. The guns are put away, so he couldn't reach one even if he tried."

"I think you should tie him up in the barn," said Abb.

Timothy patiently explained again to Abb about their vote.

Pansy grinned at Rachel. "And how did you vote?"

Rachel flushed. "Don't make trouble, Ma."

"I'm glad to see you're breaking more of that hard crust off, Rachel. One of these days I'll come over and find my soft, sweet Rachel."

"Let's go in the other room," said Rachel gruffly.

Kayla saw Rachel's embarrassment and ushered Pansy to the rocking chair Rachel usually sat in. Heat from the potbelly stove warmed the room. The chairs from the kitchen circled the room, so everyone had a place to sit. The Christmas tree stood beside Abel's rocking chair, dominating the room. Kayla could barely take her eyes off the angel. The tiny pile of gifts under the tree also intrigued her. She hadn't expected to see anything except the one for Deems, the brooch for Rachel, and the things Pansy had brought over a few days ago. The gifts were wrapped in newspaper or brown paper and tied with grocery string.

Kayla sat down on an empty chair between Timothy and Ula. Ula smiled at Kayla and gripped her hand.

Timothy leaned close to Kayla and whispered, "Abb said he and Leroy are going back to Ohio with the girls and Boon."

"Pansy will miss them," said Kayla.

Abel opened his Bible, cleared his throat, then said, "I'm going to read the Christmas story to you for the first time."

Kayla smiled at Timothy, then at Ula. Ula could barely sit still. She'd never gotten a Christmas gift before. None of the Larsens nor Abb or Leroy had either. Boon, Marigold, and Beryl had told them about some of their past gifts, and the others had listened to the stories in awe.

Kayla looked at Abel as he once again cleared his throat. She knew he felt self-conscious but was determined to make that Christmas a special day for all of them.

Abel read about the angel visiting Mary, then about the birth of Jesus.

Kayla listened to the story she knew by heart while tears stung her eyes. She glanced at Deems in a chair near the sofa and wondered if he'd ever heard the Christmas story before.

"Jesus was God's great gift to us," said Abel. "The best gift we could ever receive. It's because of Jesus that we are celebrating this special day." He grinned at Kayla and Timothy. "And it's also because of the wonderful gifts God sent us straight from Ireland."

Kayla smiled, and Timothy sat up straighter, a proud look on his face.

"We're glad for all of our guests and family." Abel smiled around the circle. "Now it's time to open our gifts." He picked up a small package. "This is for Scott."

"It's not big enough to be a sled," said Scott. "But I'll like it anyway."

Kayla held her breath as Scott ripped off the paper. Inside was a slate with words on it.

"'Look behind the sofa,'" read Scott. He turned to Abel. "Why does it say that?"

"Look and see," said Abel.

Rachel looked as eager as Scott as he ran to peer behind the sofa.

"A sled!" he cried. He pulled out the wooden sled and ran his hands lovingly over it. "A real sled! Thank you!"

Kayla clapped and cheered with the others. One by one each person opened their gifts. Pansy had made candy for each one. Jane had stitched hankies for everyone, and Ula had drawn pictures of animals for them all. Kayla gave each person a penny. She'd hesitated over giving one to Boon, but decided to give him one anyway.

Abel handed the wrapped halter to Deems. "This is from Timothy and Kayla."

Deems flushed, then reluctantly took the package. "I don't know what to say," he said with a catch in his voice.

"No need to say anything," said Abel.

Kayla locked her hands in her lap as Deems slowly tore off the paper and lifted up the halter.

"It's for Sill," said Timothy.

Deems cleared his throat and dashed tears from his eyes. "He'll wear it with pride. Thank you."

Finally it was time for Abel to give his gift to Rachel. Slowly he pulled it out of his pocket where he'd slipped it earlier. "This is for you, Rachel, with all my love."

Rachel fought against the tears, but one slipped down her cheek as she took the gift. "I don't know why you'd want to bother."

"You deserve more than that," said Abel, smiling at her.

Kayla's heart hammered so loud she was sure everyone heard it. She wanted Rachel to like the brooch.

Rachel tore off the paper, then gasped as she stared down at the silver and amethyst brooch. She held it to her heart and couldn't speak. "It's . . . it's beautiful," she finally whispered. She tried to pin it to the high neck of her dark-green wool dress, but her hands shook so badly she finally gave up. She walked to Abel and knelt at his chair. "Will you do it, Abel?"

He took the brooch, kissed Rachel, then pinned the brooch in place. "Merry Christmas," he said softly.

"Merry Christmas," she said.

Kayla closed her eyes and felt the love surround her. She smiled and turned to Timothy. "Merry Christmas," she whispered.

"Merry Christmas, Kayla O'Brian. Next year at this time may you have what you want most. And may I be tall and strong."

"You're a fine brother, Timothy!"

He puffed out his chest and his blue eyes twinkled. "That I am!"

Kayla laughed. Then suddenly her stomach growled with hunger. Smells of the Christmas goose drifted in from the kitchen.

Just then Rachel walked out of the room. Everyone grew very quiet. Kayla moved uneasily. Was Rachel going to tell them the party was over and now it was time to get back to work? Even Abel looked a little nervous.

Rachel walked back into the front room, a large platter in her hands. She held her head high and smiled. "I have a gift for everyone," she said.

Kayla gasped along with everyone else. "Don't go thinking you're the only ones that can do something special for Christmas," said Rachel. "I stayed up last night making the gifts."

"You're a fine woman," said Abel with a soft laugh. Flushing, Rachel lowered the platter. On it were sugar cookies decorated in red and green. Rachel had written a name on each cookie. "You may take your cookie now, eat it, or save it for later."

"They're real nice, Rachel," said Pansy.

"They are!" cried the others.

Smiling, Rachel walked around the room, holding the platter down for each one to reach. Kayla found her cookie and picked it up.

"Thank you, Rachel," Kayla said with a smile.

"Thank you," said Timothy as he took his cookie.

"I'm glad God sent you to us," Rachel said softly.

"Me too," said Timothy and Kayla in one voice.

Kayla looked at her cookie, then slowly took a tiny

nibble. It was the best-tasting cookie she'd ever had. She took another bite, then another.

But she saved her name, the name Rachel had written so carefully. She'd eat that much later.